SWINE AND PUNISHMENT

ELLEN RIGGS

BOUGHT-THE-FARM
MYSTERIES

FREE PREQUEL

Rescuing this pup could bring Ivy a whole new life... if it doesn't kill her first.

Discover how big city executive Ivy meets Keats, her crime-solving sheepdog, in A Dog with Two Tales. Ivy Galloway doesn't know how desperate she is to escape the big city and her soul-sucking corporate career until she meets a sheepdog in need of rescue, too. This short prequel to the laugh-out-loud Bought-the-Farm Mystery series is a page-turner for lovers of animals, humor and spunky amateur sleuths. Join Ellen Riggs' author newsletter at **ellenriggs.com/opt-in** to get this FREE prequel.

Swine and Punishment

ISBN 978-1-998742-01-1 Paperback - D2D
ISBN 978-1-989303-64-1 eBook
ISBN 978-1-990613-21-0 AudioBook
ASIN B08F4LHZ52 Kindle
ASIN 1989303633 Paperback
ASIN B0CT465182 AudioBook

Publisher: Ellen Riggs
www.ellenriggs.com
Cover designer: Lou Harper
Editor: Serena Clarke
2501221643

CHAPTER ONE

Percy jumped down from my shoulder, gave a yodeling howl, and doubled in size with an explosive puff of long fur. The marmalade tabby normally served as an ambassador for Runaway Farm and Inn, but he'd finally found a guest he didn't like.

"Be a gentleman, Percy," I said, as he arched his back and started a strange sideways dance across the snow-covered gravel driveway. He moved like a tarantula, and I had no doubt he'd pack a poisonous punch if he reached his target. "You gave up feral life months ago."

"Maybe I should grab his carry bag from the truck and take him inside," Jilly Blackwood said. My best friend was a confirmed cat lover, but she had her limits.

"Good luck with that. He's going to slice and dice whatever stands in his way." I looked around and saw my know-it-all sheepdog sitting on his haunches and watching the spectacle. His mouth hung open in a dog smirk and he panted a ha-ha-ha. "Don't just sit there, Keats. It's your professional obligation to make sure everyone feels safe and comfortable here."

"Unless they're murderers," Jilly said, grinning.

"There's an exception to every rule," I said. "And Evie Spring-dale is the opposite of a murderer. She's a lifesaver and rescuer."

This was quite literally true. Evie was part of a rescue brigade from Dorset Hills, the bigger and more prosperous city next door to our town, Clover Grove. She regularly saved the lives of dogs, cats and other animals, and was married to a veterinarian, too.

"In Percy's defense, Evie isn't the problem," Jilly said. "Whatever possessed her to bring Roberto along?"

Evie was still gathering her things while Roberto, her shorthaired ginger tabby, pressed his face to the rear window of the sedan. Judging by his open mouth and splayed claws, Roberto was neither impressed nor cowed by Percy's unseemly display. Turning, Evie spoke to her cat and then shrugged at Jilly and me. She couldn't get out without either releasing Roberto or welcoming Percy. My cat was fully capable of slipping through a crack like a harsh wind and blowing things up from inside. He was an elite sneak and professional stowaway.

"This meeting is important so we need a solution fast." I turned again. "Keats, I'm looking at you."

If a dog had shoulders, he'd have shrugged. While Keats and Percy were the best of frenemies, the canine genius didn't fully grasp feline ways. Neither did I, but we were all learning.

Evie had offered to help us come up with a marketing strategy to attract more guests to the inn following an unfortunate series of murders on or around the farm. The incidents had nothing to do with me or the inn but no one remembered that. I could only stay afloat because Hannah Pemberton, the billionaire heiress who'd previously owned the farm, continued to subsidize the business. Our luck had improved since Christmas, however. Three different sets of guests had come and gone without mishap—all based on the recommendation of Clover Grove's mayor who had stayed with us over the holiday.

Evie rolled down her window a bit. "I thought this would be fun. Did you know Roberto helped me crack an exotic pet ring in Dorset

Hills? He's a hero. So, I figured the two cats had something in common. Other than being orange."

It was hard to hear her over the screeching. Now Percy was standing with his paws against the back door of the car, menacing Roberto from close range.

"Enough already," I said. "I'm going in."

That finally propelled Keats to action. He wouldn't intervene of his own accord, but if my welfare was at stake he felt obligated.

We walked over to the car together. I stuck out my boot, hooked Percy around the middle and gently dislodged him from the car. He turned and spit in my direction.

"That doesn't sound good," Evie said.

I stared down at the cat, unflinching. "Percy, we've talked about your cattitude. I can and will bench you from all team activities if you carry on like this. Do you want to spend your days hunting for mice like the barn cats? Because those are your choices. We all contribute around here."

Jilly crossed her arms in solidarity. "Normally, I take your side, Percy. I got you a coat and a travel bag, and hauling you around everywhere is making me lopsided. But hospitality is paramount here."

The cat's green eyes widened and he meowed in a more conciliatory tone.

"That's better," I said. "Go into the barn and collect yourself. You can come out and meet Roberto when you cool down."

Percy turned and walked toward the barn, tail lashing furiously. When he disappeared inside I signaled Evie that it was safe to join us.

She opened the door and there was a flash of orange as Roberto launched like a rocket. A similar missile shot out the barn door. Keats spun in a circle, confused about his best move.

It didn't matter. The cats had a meeting of the minds mid-point in their trajectories and turned as one to charge the dog instead. He threw me a resentful look with his eerie blue eye before the three animals streaked up the driveway. The cats were fast but the deep snow gave the dog a big advantage.

"Roberto, leave that dog alone," Evie yelled.

"He'll be okay," I said. "Keats has moves."

"What just happened there?" she asked. "First they're issuing death threats and then they're a team. Did we just get played?"

"Typical barnyard antics," I said. "Best to ignore them and go into the barn. They'll get nosy about what we're doing and come around." Evie started to follow and that's when I noticed the phone in her hand was discreetly aimed in my direction. "Are you filming all this?"

Pushing back the hood of her parka, she released a cloud of strawberry curls. Her pretty, lightly freckled face broke into a smile. "Who me? Why would I do that?"

"I don't know. Maybe you want to show Hannah the mayhem around here."

My worry must have been audible because Evie's smile turned from sly to kind. "Hannah knows exactly what it's like here. It was even crazier in her time." She stared around. "Without the homicide, of course."

"Then why would you film me during a visit to chat about marketing?"

"And why wouldn't you warn us?" Jilly asked, smoothing her own unruly curls. "So we could dress for the camera?"

"That's just the thing," Evie said. "People crave authenticity these days. They like you guys because your media presence isn't glossed up and staged."

"I don't have a media presence," I said. "I learned during my HR career that everything posted online comes back to bite you in the butt. All we have is a website for the inn."

As we walked into the barn, warmth closed around us like a blanket. We all unzipped our parkas. I was wearing my usual overalls over long johns and Jilly was in jeans and a cable knit sweater. Evie, on the other hand, looked chic in black pants and matching cashmere. She must have forgotten the way dust, fur and hay would insinuate themselves in the fibers of her clothes.

Directing her phone around the barn, Evie smiled. "Just because you haven't deliberately built an online presence doesn't mean you don't have one. In fact, there's nothing better than an organic following. I was pleasantly surprised to see how many views there are of the singing donkey."

"He doesn't sing anymore," I said, as she walked over to get a close-up of Bocelli. His loud, grating braying during my Christmas stint with the town choir had also led to a short feature on local TV. "That all ended when I figured out what he wanted."

Evie gave me a significant look. "It was an amazing story, Ivy. Stories move people. And stories drive business."

"No, Evie," I said. "Uh-uh. You're not doing an online show starring *this* hobby farmer like you did with Hannah Pemberton."

"Why not? You said you'd keep an open mind about my marketing ideas. The Princess and the Pig had a cult following that kept this farm going when it was at risk of being shut down. People still contact me about it every single day."

"That's because Hannah was an elegant heiress. A fish out of water. They came to watch a pig take her down a peg."

"News flash," Evie said, walking from stall to stall filming. "You're a fish out of water here, too. Think about the hook: 'Uptight exec lands in manure with the love of her life.' The same viewers will love seeing the pig take *you* down a peg."

"The love of my life will hate this idea more than you can possibly imagine," I said. "As chief of police, Kellan Harper has to keep some dignity."

Evie turned with her phone. "I meant the *true* love of your life."

Keats was now sitting in a circle of light. It gleamed off his fluffy black ears and shiny coat. His blue eye fixed Evie with a calculating stare while his warm brown eye welcomed the camera. When his mouth opened in a happy pant, his verdict was in.

"Once again, no," I said. "No to you, Evie, and no to the canine love of my life." I glanced at Jilly, expecting her to chime in with agreement.

Instead, my best friend gave a shrug. "We've got to consider all the options, Ivy. At the rate you bring in new rescue animals, your ark will sink otherwise."

"Traitor," I said.

The cats strolled in together and I had no doubt Roberto had sold Percy on the benefits of being a media darling. It was five against one, but they all underestimated my loathing for the spotlight. I'd deliberately flown under the radar my entire life. That had served me well in my 10-year career at Flordale Corporation and even more so since moving here and starting to solve mysteries. Inviting cameras to track my every move wouldn't just embarrass me and jeopardize my relationship with Kellan, it could put me at risk from the deadbeats who popped up with some regularity in Clover Grove and gravitated to me. A sleuth with an entourage couldn't solve the riddles of the day.

"Just hear me out," Evie said. "I'm thinking of something different from The Princess and the Pig. That was more of a slice-of-life reality show. Your show would be staged to deliver a very specific message."

Sensing I was too grumpy to speak, Jilly asked, "And that message is...?"

"That Runaway Inn is *the* destination for city folk craving the quaint farm and small-town experience. Jilly, you'd be inside, showing us how to prepare your stupendous meals. You'd be preserving and canning. Finding new ways to use all those eggs. Meanwhile, Ivy would be out here showing us the mysteries of manure management and talking about livestock and rescue work.

I'm seeing this show as educational. Your former careers gave you the presence to teach."

I shook my head. "So you really mean *edutainment*. I'd spout some facts about farm life while people wait for the money shot where I get trampled or bitten. Sound about right?"

Evie grinned. "Those moments are gifts to the viewers. You have to add a little sugar to the education pill if you want them to swallow."

My head was still shaking, apparently of its own accord. "Nope. Never. Not a chance."

Jilly's green eyes were alight with edutaining possibilities. She'd always been a natural teacher and gracious host. "Maybe think on it, Ivy. You know how important it is to control the message. Right now, the message is controlling us."

"Fine. I'll think on it." I walked through the back door with Keats at my heels, whining. "Not you too, buddy. You know we need to stay undercover. How would we do that with cameras following our every move?"

I pulled in some deep breaths of the frosty air. January had been the coldest month on record in hill country and February showed no sign of relenting. It had been hard, but not as bad as I feared. Farming didn't allow much time for weather angst.

Leaning against the fence bordering Wilma's pasture, I stared at the sly, stubborn sow who'd also kept Hannah on her toes. The pig had grown a thick coat because she far preferred being out here to mixing with her barnyard colleagues inside. She was a confirmed loner. I'd rotated in other livestock to give her a companion and it always ended badly. There was a reason the pig poker—a long pole with a metal hook on the end—stood ready by the gate.

A movement at the far end of the pasture caught my eye. It also caught Wilma's eye and a feral twinkle appeared. Evie's ginger cat was strolling casually around the rim of the food trough. Taunting the pig.

"Roberto, no!" I grabbed the pole and slipped through the gate. Keats shot in after me and tried to head Wilma off at the pass. The pig was surprisingly agile and extremely smart. Keats had already practiced his best herding moves on her and she'd calculated countermoves. Now, when he feinted left, she turned on a dime and charged the cat. "Jump, Roberto! Jump."

The cat either didn't understand me like Percy did or enjoyed staring down death. No one came between Wilma and her trough.

All I could do was try. Swinging the poker over my shoulder, I raced after Wilma. The smooth wooden pole quickly slid off my parka, spiraled and jammed between my boots.

It felt like I did a cartwheel but that may have only been my brain rattling loose in my skull. It hadn't been properly anchored since the head injury I sustained rescuing Keats. Either way, I ended up flat on my back in the churned-up muddy snow, staring at the gray sky. A wet nose touched my cheek and Keats poured a little sympathy into me with his brown eye while my lungs refilled. Wilma came back and stood over me, too.

"Cut!" Evie said. "Bravo, Ivy, bravo!" She came toward me with the phone in one hand and the pig poker in the other. "You can't stage moments like that. Pure gold."

Pure orange, more like. Roberto was waltzing along the top rung with his tail in the air, while Percy did the same from the other end. They met in the middle and exchanged what appeared to be a congratulatory head butt.

Scrambling to my feet, I said, "That was *not* edutainment, Evie Springdale."

"Sure it was. It was all about the wrong way to approach a testy pig. First you show that, and then you show a better way. All the while the banner promoting the inn unfurls underneath. Right?"

"Wrong," I said, stomping toward the gate. "I hope that's not your only idea."

"Just the best one," she called after me. "Fair warning, Ivy. If you don't do it, someone else will. It's in the zeitgeist. I feel it."

She'd spent nearly as much time in political PR as I had in corporate HR. I believed her. In fact, the truth of her words stung me like the fierce wind.

But I still couldn't do it. The show would have to go on without me.

CHAPTER TWO

"You said no?" Teri Mason tried to hide her disappointment and failed. I'd dropped by her art store, Hill Country Designs, expecting sympathy. I'd missed our chats during her month-long trip to Key West. There wasn't a hint of tan on her angular face, but the tropical paintings lined up against the wall suggested she'd at least spent time under a beach umbrella.

"Of course I said no." I zipped up my parka again to leave in a huff. "It would be horrible having a camera crew documenting my every move. I'm an introvert."

"I get that," Teri said. "You couldn't even blow your nose in peace."

"Exactly. The nation does not need to see that."

Keats sat between us, head swiveling to catch each of us with his sharp blue eye.

"Except I'm sure Evie Springdale would edit out the nose blowing. She sounds like a good person. Hannah Pemberton trusted her, and she didn't trust just anyone. I could hardly get a word out of Hannah when she was in here and I found her intimidating. But one time she brought in the camera crew and I can't even tell you how many calls I got after the show aired. It was the best PR ever."

"Ah. So that's why you're thinking I should take my chances with the nationwide nose blowing."

"Global, more like." Teri grinned. "The Internet knows no limits."

I looked around the empty shop. This time of year was typically slow for anyone in town who didn't sell essential supplies. "So a show would be good for business."

"Yeah. *Your* business." She smoothed her purple speckled caftan, which looked brand new. "The rest of us might see an uptick, too."

"Sorry, Teri. I can't slice open my life for the public. I attract too much attention around here as it is." I didn't try to hide my shudder. "I spent my whole life trying to escape notice and succeeded till lately. Returning to anonymity is my greatest ambition."

"I understand. Totally." Teri went around the counter and started rearranging a display of bracelets with rainbows of handmade beads. Most of her work was tailored to the average client who wanted average things, despite the fact that she had quirky taste herself.

"But you think I made the wrong decision," I said.

Keats started to pant, and not a happy ha-ha-ha. More like an anxious uh-uh-oh.

Twirling a bracelet on her index finger, Teri shook her head. "I wouldn't want cameras following me around. And it's not my place to tell you what to do."

"But...?"

The bracelet spun off her finger and soared toward me. I caught it in one hand and slipped it over my wrist.

"You see those beads?" she asked. "Look closer."

Scattered among transparent green and blue beads were a few ugly little heads with painted faces. "Are those... zombies?"

Her face lit up. "You're the only one who's noticed. I've sold quite a few of them to nice ladies from Dorset Hills who see what they want to see."

"Well, I consider myself something of a zombie connoisseur," I said. "Jilly and I have seen every zombie flick ever made." I put the bracelet on the counter and pulled out my wallet. "I assume you're trying to make a point and the sale is just a bonus."

Now she laughed. "Definitely a bonus. What I'm trying to say is that sometimes we need to cater to the masses to make a living. Other times we can have a little subversive fun. If you trust this Evie, you could deliver the message you want and save a whole lot of animals while you're doing it."

"I'm not buying her whole 'educational not sensational' pitch. You should have seen her smile when the pig was standing over me."

"Come on, who wouldn't want to see that?" Teri poured coins into my hand. "Did you take that moment to give a sound bite about pig handling? And make a plug for rescue? From what I recall, Wilma has a sad backstory of being exploited and overbred. What a great opportunity to inform people about things like that."

"That's my zombie among the jewels?" I asked. "Not buying it, Teri."

Escorting me to the door, she handed me a little brown bag. "You already did, my friend. And you'll smile every time you see it."

***

"YOU SAID NO?" Edna Evans' expression was inscrutable.

I'd bumped into her about half a block from the grocery store and we fell into step. My octogenarian neighbor usually wore her judgments with as much pride as the rabbit pelt cape draped over her shoulders. Since she became Clover Grove's official choirmaster at Christmas, however, she'd softened some of her many edges. At least on the surface. It was possible that her coat concealed the practical bulletproof vest of the apocalyptic prepper she really was. Either that or she was packing more than her usual pepper spray in her purse.

"Of course I said no. Can you imagine having a camera crew crawling all over and exposing my every move?" I shook my head. "I'm surprised you had to ask."

"I'm surprised you didn't call a team meeting to discuss the pros and cons. We might have had valuable input. I mean the *full* team, including everyone who's saved your life at least once." She held out her gloved hands and started counting. "Some of us don't have enough fingers."

I held up two fingers. "Twice, in your case."

"Directly, maybe. I've put my life on the line for you plenty more fingers than that."

It was true that Edna was always willing to put herself on the line when there was trouble of the murderous kind. Whether she was courageous or crazy was still up for debate. Probably both. Many would say the same of me.

"Okay, but why would you care?" I asked. "You already sit by your window with binoculars guarding your privacy. Like you said only recently, my problems become your problems."

She shrugged her rabbit pelts. "That was before. Now I'm prepared for anything, as you know. Besides, Evie Springdale has a good head on her shoulders. I trust her judgment."

"Evie Springdale brought her cat over to the farm when she came to make her pitch. That was good judgment?"

Another shrug of rabbits. "I'm sure she had her reasons. Roberto is a fine cat."

"She wanted to create conflict, which creates good TV. But her plan backfired. She got the footage and also a hard no."

"A hard no never helps negotiations," she said. "You know that. After providing such good fodder, which I enjoyed by the way, you were in the driver's seat." Finally she smirked. "That said, your performance in the driver's seat leaves much to be desired. And that's why you call on your team to represent you."

I leaned against a stop sign and crossed my arms. "How exactly did you see what happened? The pig pen isn't in your sight line."

"I had a few trees trimmed."

"You mean a forest. I kept hearing a chainsaw and now I know why."

"To get a little exercise and keep my friends safe. Win-win."

Pushing myself off the pole, I continued to the store. "What's the win for you in my doing a reality show?"

"If it's educational and not sensational—"

"Oh my goodness! Evie put you up to this, didn't she?"

"No one manipulates Edna Evans anymore, Ivy. All that changed when—"

"I saved *your* life," I interrupted.

She grinned. "I'm still up by a handful of fingers."

"I repeat... What's in it for you?"

"I can't believe I have to explain this to you, the only smart Galloway Girl."

"That is not true. My sisters are all smart. I'm just the most educated."

"Dahlia saved her best for last. Like fireworks." Edna sighed. "I suppose your brother was such a disappointment she had to try one last time."

"Asher's a respected cop and Mom's golden boy," I said. "Anyway, that's a red herring. Just cut to the chase, Edna. I've got somewhere to be after I pick up Jilly's bay leaves."

"Stew?" Edna asked. No matter how many times Jilly made it for her, she never tired of it. "It could use some oregano."

"Red herring. Spew before stew."

She sighed. "I shouldn't have to spell this out for you, Ivy. But if cameras were crawling all over your place, it seems like your animals, your business and your friends would be safer. Then maybe I could get a good night's sleep instead of standing watch."

Her answer stopped me in my tracks. "Edna. I hope you're not exhausting yourself. You can't compromise your own health for mine."

"That's what friends do," she said. "At least that's what I observe from my role model, Keats."

Finally I smiled—at her, and then at my amazing dog. "You could do far worse, Edna. Still, there's got to be a better way. A TV show goes against everything we're trying to build with the Clover Grove Culture Revival Project. We're aiming for quaint, not crass."

She signaled for me to open the door for her and said, "My show choir could use all the press it can get."

"Aha! There *is* something in it for you."

She adjusted her pelts with a flourish so that fur whacked me as she passed. "I'll pick up the bay leaves and stop by to put in a good word with the chef."

"Do not turn Jilly against me," I called after her. "Or Percy either."

"Enjoy your last lunch without cameras, Ivy," she called over her shoulder. "You'll be the most popular gal in town."

———

"YOU SAID NO." Kellan was the first person to make it a statement, not a question. He was also the first person to sound relieved. At least I'd called one shot right.

He took my coat and hung it on the pegs just inside the door of the Berry Good Café. Then he offered his arm and led me to our favorite booth. We'd only met there twice but our dates were so few and far between that two visits qualified the spot as "our place."

"Of course I said no. I didn't consider it for a second." He waited for me to slide into the booth before taking the seat opposite. When I was with Kellan, the most handsome man in town, either fluttering butterflies or thundering goats filled my chest, depending on how much trouble I was in over intruding on his police investigations.

There had been some kind of internal disruption with Kellan in the vicinity since we were teens, except for an unfortunate 10-year hiatus. "But some of my nearest and dearest think I should be inviting cameras into my life."

"Your mother?" he said. "I could see that would be up her alley."

"I haven't spoken to Mom. I keep letting her go to voicemail." I picked up my napkin and unfolded it. "Word got around with its usual speed. You heard about it from Asher?"

He shook his head. His thick dark hair was adorably unruly from his hat. Mine just got staticky and flat.

"Betty. At the front desk."

"Bunhead Betty?" My face started to heat up remembering how Bunhead thought I was lying about being Kellan's girlfriend when I arrived at the police station with two pets and someone's femur under my arm. She thought I wasn't good enough for him and I'm sure she wasn't alone. There were many women in town who'd like to be in my place right now and they didn't make a secret of it. "How did she find out?" I held up my hand. "Scratch that. How does anyone find out anything in this town?"

He offered me the menu with a smile. "The usual?"

"The usual." I loved that we had a usual. In fact, we had burgers on most dates. Jilly fed me so well at home that I liked to stick to the slow lane when I was out. "Double fries, please."

"You can have mine," he said.

"Oh, I will. I'm a hardworking farmer who needs her carbs."

His smile lit up the room and my heart. "I like to see a gal with an appetite."

We both leaned forward and there was a high risk of a public display of affection. Instead, Kellan gave a sharp gasp.

"What?" I worried for a second that my breath was sour.

"Someone nipped my calf, that's what. Stuck his cold nose up my pant leg and caught just enough skin to— *Ow!*"

"Keats!" I pushed back the tablecloth and glared at my dog, who was all impish grins. "Stop that."

He didn't like being relegated to the basement of our date, but he was lucky to be in here at all. I carried paperwork to prove Keats was a service dog trained to help me through post-traumatic stress disorder. It was all legit. I still suffered from flashbacks from a violent attack when I rescued the pup from the criminal who owned him. No one in town really bought that, unfortunately. Service dogs and anxiety were for city girls. To be fair, I didn't help my own cause by taking on killers—and winning. These things didn't add up for people. They didn't always add up for me, either. But after Keats came into my life, things didn't need to add up anymore. They were what they were.

Kellan shifted again in his seat. "Honestly. Can't a man just enjoy a burger with his gal now and then?"

"Keats wants to keep an eye on everything. He's bored under there."

"How about a nap, like a normal dog? Wouldn't that be a nice change for him?"

"Keats doesn't nap. Sometimes he closes his eyes but I think it's just to hear better. His ears are always twitching, picking up sounds from the barn. Or another dimension." I grinned at Kellan. "Helping you keep tabs on this wonderful town of ours."

"Well, I appreciate that. I need all the help I can get."

Normally he would dismiss the very idea of needing help from a dog. He must be in a very good mood indeed over my having turned down the opportunity to televise my life.

A young blonde waitress came over and Kellan ordered for us. It was old-fashioned and courtly and I loved it. I had ordered my own meals in some of the finest restaurants in the world and now I was thrilled to have this handsome man order our burgers without even flinching over my double order of fries.

When she was gone, he reached across the table and took my left hand. My right hand was now under the table scratching a pair of ears. Keats loved that so much he might stop the siege below deck.

"It's been great, hasn't it?" Kellan asked. "How quiet it's been lately?"

"So great," I said. The furry ears jerked out of reach. The dog in the cheap seats disagreed. "We needed a rest from all that excitement."

"It's always slower in winter. Too cold for criminals."

I laughed. "Crime takes winters off in Clover Grove?"

"It pretty much does. I cleaned up a lot of cold cases last year. Hoping to do the same now. Beats going to Florida."

"Meanwhile I'm planning ahead," I said. "Charlie and I want to build a second barn and fence off more pastures."

His smile faded. "Isn't the ark already full?"

"Overflowing. Crowded livestock are testy livestock. Luckily most like being rotated outside."

"Business must be a lot better if you're expanding."

"Not barn-raising better. Yet. That's why some people think I should have said yes to Evie. They say it would bring more guests to the inn. But if it means waiting till next year to build, that's okay with me."

The waitress came back with our sodas. "Did you hear? Isn't it exciting?"

"Isn't what exciting?" Kellan asked.

She was young, barely 20, and didn't hear the concern in his voice. Keats did. His posture improved immediately under the table and his ears came forward under my fingers. Things were sounding more interesting.

"The TV show," she said. "We're all going to get a chance to be on it."

Kellan released my hand. "What TV show is that"—he checked her name tag—"Jasmine?"

The young woman looked from him to me and back, and then

her cheeks flushed. "I thought everyone knew. No one can stop talking about it."

Kellan's dark blue eyes shifted to me and I shook my head. "I missed the memo, Jasmine," he said. "Can you fill me in?"

She was already backing away as she realized that she was not only breaking news to the chief of police, but also bad news. At least to him.

"Some TV people came in here yesterday," she said. "With cameras."

By now Jasmine was halfway back to the counter and her hands fluttered as she called, "They asked about Ivy. And her dog. How often she came in. What she wore. What she ate. What Keats did when she was here."

The dog poked his head out from under the table and gave an indignant mumble. Maybe he wanted an agent.

"I don't understand," Kellan said, as Jasmine disappeared into the kitchen. "I thought you said no to this."

"I most certainly did." I pulled out my phone. "If Evie is going ahead without my permission, someone's going to be in deep manure... and for once it isn't me."

I left a voicemail for her just as the burgers arrived in the hands of the manager.

"On the house," he said. "Just remember us when you're famous." Staring down at Keats, who hadn't retreated yet, he added, "We should get the dog's photo for the wall."

Kellan pulled out his credit card. "That would send the wrong message about pets in dining establishments. And I can't accept your kind offer."

"Should we take these to go?" I asked, wondering if Kellan was too upset now to enjoy our date.

He shook his head as the manager left. "Not at all. You're going to need your fries piping hot to get to the bottom of this situation."

"I'm sure it's all a misunderstanding. There's no way news this big could have missed us."

"Good point," he said, trying to smile.

It was so forced that I knew we were now in the market for a new place to call ours.

CHAPTER THREE

I was slip-sliding along Main Street when Evie finally called me back. My boots had terrific treads but staying upright was challenging without full-on cleats these days. Yet if I wore cleats, I slid around inside stores. There was no winning in this town.

"First, not guilty," Evie said. "I might have been guilty in sleezier political times, but now I'm one of the good guys, remember?"

"I know you are, and I told Kellan that, too. But there's a TV crew hanging around Clover Grove asking questions about me." Keats mumbled something at my side. "And about Keats, too. He's a celebridog."

"I don't know what any of this means," Evie said, "but it's just a matter of time till I find out. I've contacted every friend in film and media." There was a pause as her phone pinged. "Hang on. Oh. Oh no."

A big pile of fries flipflopped in my gut. "Oh no *what?*"

"Someone's already stolen your thunder," she said. "A mid-sized network is doing a reality show about a former executive who runs a hobby farm and inn. They're shooting some scenes on location in Clover Grove."

I let out a strangled squawk that startled a senior citizen. I reached out just in time to stop her from falling and it felt like we were waltzing for a second. My phone hit the icy pavement and the woman accidentally kicked it a few yards. I could hear Evie yelling, "Ivy? Ivy! Are you okay?" Her words were muffled by Keats' mouth as he retrieved the phone and carried it back.

The woman not only ignored my apology but also gave me a dirty look before going on her way. As if I'd choose to hug a grumpy stranger on Main Street.

I took the phone from Keats and rubbed the saliva off with one glove before holding it to my ear.

"I'm here. I'm fine. Mostly." Pushing my hat out of my eyes, I said, "Tell me more about this reality show."

"Are you sure you want to know?"

"I don't want to know, but I need to know. If they're prying into my life."

"Well, the show's working title is 'Faraway Farm.' My friend sent a graphic and the 'm' is falling off the sign."

The old iron sign over my lane read "Runaway Far" because the "m" had long since rusted out.

"Are you kidding me? They're *copying* my life? They didn't even ask me. Don't I get a say?"

I didn't need to see her head shaking to know it was happening. "They'll say any resemblance is pure coincidence. Or that the show is inspired by you and Hannah and others. City girls who bite off more than they can chew with a farm."

"I was born and raised in Clover Grove, remember."

"Then maybe they'll position it as a homecoming homesteader," she said. "I don't have all the details yet."

"This is ridiculous. I'll sue them." Keats and I crossed at the last corner and I deliberately slowed to finish the conversation before reaching my destination. "Do you have a good lawyer?"

"Sure, but they'll say shows like these are experts at avoiding litigation. They'll say that ideas can't be copyrighted. That it was in the zeitgeist, which I told you."

I plucked off my hat and threw it at a parking meter. "They've practically stolen the farm's name, and they're asking about what I eat and wear. Isn't that proof it's about me? What if they start asking about my other activities?"

"Of the crimefighting variety?" Evie asked. "They'd be walking on very thin ice. Kellan would put a stop to that."

"Can't you do something, Evie?" Keats brought back my hat, too. He held onto it long enough to infuse me with calm from his warm brown eye.

"All I can do is keep the lines of communication open with my contacts and gather information. You know Cori is going to freak when she hears this. The last thing anyone needs is a camera crew popping up unexpectedly." Evie laughed lightly. "Unless I'm directing of course."

Cori Hogan shared leadership of the Rescue Mafia with Bridget Linsmore and they were no strangers to lawbreaking when it came to saving animals. They were already cautious about coming to the farm because of Kellan and Asher, although a reciprocal exchange of incriminating information had thawed what began as chilly antagonism.

"Is it too late?" I asked. "Could we take control of the message by staging our own show?"

I could sense her red curls shaking again at the other end. "They beat us to the punch, Ivy. We may just be hearing about it now but they've been working on it for months, I bet. Plus they have a big budget. I should have pitched you long ago but I was so sure you'd say no. And now someone's stolen your thunder."

"My thunder? They've stolen my life." I looked down at Keats and sighed. "Probably wasn't easy finding a border collie with one blue eye."

Evie finally laughed. "They'll just pop a contact lens onto any old dog. There's nothing real about reality television."

After saying goodbye and hanging up, I shook my head. "Did you hear that, buddy? Even you can be faked."

I opened the door and he made a big show of rolling his blue eye at me as he passed. They could fake me, they could fake my farm, but we both knew they could never fake a dog like Keats.

CHAPTER FOUR

"Darling," Mom said as I stepped into Bloomers, the unisex salon she ran with my sister, Iris. "I've called you half a dozen times."

"Make that thirty," I said, waving to Iris, who was behind the counter working on a laptop. "I reported you to the police for harassment."

"Oh, you poor thing," Mom said, starting to wipe down her red vinyl barbershop chair with disinfectant. "You still think you're funny. It's so strange with all that's happened." She tossed me a wry smile. "How many murders will it take?"

"Humor's all that keeps me going sometimes. Aside from my manure pile."

I didn't bother unzipping my parka before collapsing into the other empty styling chair. Like the crime business, pampering dropped off in winter. On the whole, though, their joint venture was going well.

Mom straightened and rested one hand on the hip of her monogrammed Bloomers smock. "Please don't go on about dung explosions when the cameras are rolling. The rest of the Galloways deserve better."

"Our family name is already mud," Iris said. "Oddly, it helps business. People come in to see if we're as crazy as the rumors."

"We're not, are we, handsome?" Mom asked Keats as he pranced in front of her, white paws pumping. He didn't court attention often but he had plenty of love to spare for the biggest thorn in my side. "Although I suppose a whiff of crazy makes for good TV."

"How'd you hear about the show?" I asked. "Clients?"

"Jilly, of course," Mom said, going back to her cleaning. When I was growing up she'd left all matters of hygiene to my eldest sister, Daisy. Now that she had her own business, Mom was always buffing and polishing like a guy with a collectible car. After all the jobs she'd cycled through, it was a relief to see her thriving. "She said you turned down Evie Springdale but people are talking about camera crews, so I assume you changed your mind. Sounds like you made the right decision even without my help."

I used one boot to spin my chair and Mom bent over to mop up the water and salt I'd left behind. "I said no to Evie, but there's another show coming to town. It's called Faraway Farm and features a former executive turned hobby farmer. She cooks, too, according to Evie's grapevine. Sounds like the star is Jilly and me rolled into one."

Mom froze with her cloth on the floor and Iris stopped tapping the keyboard. The lull before the storm.

"Pardon me?" Mom shot out the comment as she stood up. Her eyes narrowed into hazel slits. "Are you saying this production is—?"

"Based on my life, apparently. Suddenly Hollywood has recognized the appeal of homesteading."

"But that's outrageous! How are they compensating you for this?"

"All I can hope for is that they leave me alone while they're reimagining my life in a studio somewhere. I assume they'll only show up for some exterior footage. The town's already atwitter."

"How are we the last to know?" Mom said.

Iris came around the counter. "Because people walk on eggshells around us. They never know when you're going to blow up, Mom."

"Blow up!" Mom directed her spray bottle at Iris. "I am the model of professionalism in this salon."

I snorted. "You threatened someone with a straightedge razor in this salon, Mom."

"Why is it you kids only remember occasional misfires? I've done plenty right in my life, too. Like producing the original Ivy Rose Galloway. And if someone's blatantly stealing your identity, you need to sue."

It made more sense to let things go. To pretend it wasn't happening. Protesting would only attract more attention.

"If they think farm life is so fascinating, they can knock themselves out," I said, placing a still-snowy boot on her barbershop chair as a circuit-breaker. Mom's loop would repeat endlessly, otherwise. She was like a flustered hen when she got going—pecking and flapping until she forgot the original cause. "Evie said they've cast a midlist actress as lead. If she has delusions of sweet country life, I guarantee it will not end well for her."

Mom shoved my boot off her chair with enough force to make me slide off my own seat. I caught myself before my butt hit the footrest and ended up on the floor in the puddle she hadn't finished mopping. Keats circled around me, mumbling anxiously.

"You okay?" Iris asked, coming over.

"Yeah yeah. I do worse all the time," I said. "I'm fine, Keats. Why so worried?"

The dog was panting and it wasn't the happy one. His ears flicked back and forth and then he went into a point just before the door opened. A cold wind hit me in the face and chilled the water beneath me.

Standing in the doorway was a tall woman backed by two men, each of whom had a camera resting on one shoulder. I stayed where I was. If I wanted to keep a low profile, it couldn't get much lower than this.

"Hello, everyone," the woman said. Her voice was rich and melodious. Professionally trained, no doubt. "I'm Vivian Crane. Perhaps you've heard of me?"

"No," we all said at once, and Keats added his voice to the chorus.

"Really?" Vivian sounded incredulous. "The Cupcake Millionaire? Find That Diamond?"

Mom spoke up. "Are those... stores?"

"TV shows." A smaller woman stepped forward. She reminded me a bit of Cori Hogan, with short dark hair and a sporty Audrey Hepburn look. "I'm Becky Bower, Vivian's producer. She has a huge following in the reality show space."

"I don't watch TV," Mom said. "But welcome to Clover Grove. I'm Dahlia Galloway, and these are my daughters, Iris and Ivy." She turned to me. "Get up, darling. We have guests."

Mom stepped a little closer, taking Vivian's measure. The actress was of similar vintage to Mom, with a shiny dark bob, striking blue eyes, and a very slim build. She was wearing a gorgeous purple coat, with a matching ruffled scarf, and heels to beat Mom at her best.

Stepping back again, Mom slithered out of her Bloomer's smock. Under it, she was wearing a red knit dress and matching pumps. Somehow, despite the other woman's glamor, my petite mother managed to rival her presence. But then, all the world was a stage for Dahlia Galloway.

"What can we do for you today, Vivian?" Iris asked. "Hair? Nails? Or just some product?"

"We have a wardrobe department," Vivian said. "Such as it is. These shows never have a big enough budget, but I make do."

"We're here scouting locations for Vivian's new show," Becky said. "It's called Faraway Farm."

Mom made a choking sound and clutched her throat. It looked

theatrical but sounded legit. "Is this the show we've been hearing about that's modeled on Ivy's life?" She gestured to me, still seated in the puddle with my arm now wrapped around Keats, who had the faintest hint of a growl rolling in his chest.

"Not at all," Becky said, creating a human barrier in front of Vivian. "Although we enjoyed the videos of Ivy and the donkey singing Christmas carols."

"Absolutely adorable," Vivian said. "The network was looking for something fresh and charming, with a Hallmark feel to it. I'm known for my cooking, entertaining and décor, so it was a perfect fit."

"A perfect fit?" Mom stood a little taller but fell far short of meeting Vivian eye to eye. "My daughter, whose life you're stealing, is half your age."

"Hardly," Vivian said, evaluating me. "Rest assured, my character is a mix of all the happy homesteaders flooding social media. People crave simplicity and comfort in these difficult times."

"Farming is far from simple," I said, from my seat on the floor. "It's the most complicated thing I've ever done. But maybe that's just me."

"Tell us more, Ivy," Becky said. "In fact, we'd love to have you on board as a consultant. We don't have a lot of farming experience."

One of the cameramen snickered. "Make that none."

He was tall and attractive if you liked the arty type, with a wisp of a goatee and a swoop of dark hair that kept falling in his eyes.

"Ray," Becky said. "Enough. You too, Eric."

Ray exchanged a look with Eric, who was at least a decade older and had probably worked in the sun too much. It was clear that they didn't enjoy their place in the pecking order.

"Thanks, Becky, but I'm afraid I've got too much work on my hands as it is," I said.

"We'd negotiate a fair fee," Becky continued. "Enough to offset some of your problems on the farm."

Keats mumbled something and I nodded. "How kind of you, but all is well at Runaway Farm. Lots of people will be thrilled, though. Your show will attract attention to our humble town. More power to you."

Mom turned again and glared at me. "Get up and face these people right now. They're stealing your life and selling it and you're just sitting there clutching your dog like a teddy bear."

I looked straight at Ray's lens. "Mom gets a little riled when she's defending her family."

"Sometimes she even turns *on* the family," Iris added.

Mom threw up her hands in disgust. "Ivy, speak up. Earlier you said, 'If she wants to steal my sweet country life, I guarantee it will not end well for her.'"

"Mom!" I pushed myself up off the floor and initiated damage control. "All I said was that anyone with delusions of sweet country life might get a rude wake-up call. It's mostly dirty, hard work. My day starts and ends with manure. Do they pay you enough, Vivian?"

"Oh, it won't be like that for me," she said. Her blue eyes were alight now that I was on my feet and providing the conflict Evie told me every show needed to keep viewers' attention. "Nearly everything takes place in studio and we've done a lot of shooting already."

Becky moved around Mom and beckoned the guys. I turned at the same time to keep my eyes on the camera.

"The props team is making over our exterior location here in town right now," Vivian said. "We've leased a century-old farmhouse and they're building a barn."

"What house is that?" I asked, suspicion dawning. Keats' ruff had come up and his ears flattened.

"It belonged to someone named Vinnie Swenson," Becky said. "I believe you met recently." She gave Ray a signal that was probably a request to zoom in on my reaction.

"Vinnie passed before I could meet him," I said. "But I did inherit Bocelli, his wonderful donkey. The one you've seen online.

And a miniature horse named Clippers. So I think rather fondly of Vinnie, despite the supposedly colorful life he led."

"I do hope you'll come for our launch party," Vivian said. "And bring your chef. Billy Whitewater, I believe."

"Jilly Blackwood," I corrected. "I wish we could, but we're so busy. Running a real farm and inn is nonstop work."

Vivian started circling and I rotated, too. Now the camera crew managed to slip behind me.

"Is this the famous dog I've heard so much about?" Vivian asked.

"This is Keats. My sheepdog. Couldn't run the farm without him."

Normally he loved a compliment but he was spinning, too, trying to keep an eye on Vivian and the crew.

"It can't be," Vivian said, crouching to take a closer look at the dog. His ears were still back and he turned the full force of his eerie blue eye on her. It didn't faze the star one bit. She glanced up at Becky. "You got the wrong dog. Again. That beast is four times the size."

"It's a sheepdog," Becky said. "Or so the breeder said."

"There are lots of herding breeds," I said. "Keats is a border collie."

"Oh Becky, seriously," Vivian said. "The dog is critical to the show. If you can't get a simple thing like that right, how can I trust you for anything?"

Becky wilted. "We'll get him a blue contact lens. It'll be fine."

"So then we'll have a blue-eyed bear?" Vivian grumbled as they all headed for the door. "I'm surrounded by incompetents."

Becky held the door for Vivian, who called back, "See you at the launch, Ivy. Mayor Martingale put you on the list. She's been wonderful about all this, and the network is very pleased about the tax breaks."

"I hope it goes well for you," I called, directing a bright smile at Ray, who was already lowering his camera.

"Did you get the jeans?" Becky asked him as they left the salon.

"Oh, Ivy," Mom said, as I tried to look over my shoulder. "It looks like you wet your pants. What will people think?"

"I'm tired of worrying about what people think." I looked down at Keats and sighed. "See, I knew they couldn't fake *you*, buddy."

CHAPTER FIVE

In the parking lot at the late Vinnie Swenson's place, Daisy, Iris and Violet orbited Mom as if she'd been named Planet Dahlia. Keeping her out of trouble at the launch of the Faraway Farm show was going to be a bigger challenge than pretending this whole situation didn't annoy the heck out of me. I suspected Becky and her crew would be tailing me throughout the event for reaction shots. I'd even considered leaving Keats at home to deny them access. Our relationship was mostly private and completely magical—at least in the day-to-day sense of the word—and I didn't want to share a single moment of his time. In the end, I couldn't leave him behind because I needed help to play *my* role today. This would be one of my bigger tests since leaving Flordale Corp, where my talent for downsizing staff and destroying their lives had gained me the nickname "Grim Reaper."

"It'll be fine," Jilly said. She'd put extra care into her hair, makeup and outfit but her expression was bleak. "Game face on."

"Back at you," I said. "Let's remember our HR roots. Bland. Ordinary. Emotionless."

"Like robots?" The voice made me jump but it shouldn't have.

Edna Evans had become a master of stealth in the months since we met. "You're planning to bore the cameras so they go away?"

"That's the general idea," I said. "You look nice, Edna. Are you going to try for a little face time with Vivian to drop the choir into conversation?"

"If I can get something out of this I will," she said. "I doubt they'll last long. The first whiff of manure will send them running. Reality reeks, at least in my experience."

Jilly and I laughed and it did us a world of good. Keats, too. His tail came up and his ears and nose twitched. The place seemed to smell pretty fine to him.

"I keep thinking about what happened the last time we were here," I said, glancing toward the old barn. It still looked like the wreck that had housed Vinnie's neglected livestock and, eventually, his earthly remains.

"Look forward, not back," Edna said, taking my elbow and turning me by force. "That's all any of us can do. Life always holds some surprises."

What we saw in front of us was most definitely a surprise. The house had been in good shape before but now it was decked out with stately urns full of hardy winter shrubs trimmed with ribbon in seasonally neutral colors. All the wood trim was freshly painted, and there was a doll hanging on the front door that was supposed to look quaint but gave me the creeps.

"See that doll?" I said. "It's a zombie baby. The apocalypse just got one step closer, Edna."

"Don't play on an old woman's hopes," she said, propelling me up the driveway with one hand and Jilly with the other. "I'm sure nothing that dramatic will happen today. But if it does, rest assured I'm prepared. My go kit is in your truck and you can depend on me, girls."

Jilly held one gloved finger to her lips and whispered, "Stop it, you two. We need to act normal today, remember?"

"But you're the only normal one," I said. "Edna and I are the opposite of normal."

She laughed again. "Only my HR training has let me fool you so long. Trust me, I come from a long line of eccentrics."

Jilly hadn't shared much about her family since we met in college, but I knew she was happy to leave them behind and hadn't gone home for years. In fact, our shared determination to put family behind us had drawn us together and it was ironic that my family had not only stepped to center stage in my life but happily adopted Jilly. It was only a matter of time before my brother made that official. She was already everyone's favorite Galloway.

"Why am I only hearing about these eccentrics now?" I said. "More importantly, when can I meet them?"

"Probably sooner than I'd like," she said. "Your social media following exposed my whereabouts and the calls have started again."

I had my own worries about that. Just before Christmas, Asher had revealed that our deadbeat father was alive and well, and possibly lurking in the wings. I hoped he wouldn't reappear to try warming up the very cold embers of our family relationship.

Keats stopped swiveling long enough to thrust his soft ears under my fingertips. "I'm okay, buddy. Just keep that sniffer going and let us know if we have anything to worry about."

"What would there be to worry about?" Edna said. "It's just a silly TV show."

I shivered, and it wasn't from the cold. "It's Percy," I said. "He keeps trampling this place and covering it with invisible cat litter. I mean, in the ceramic version of Clover Grove."

"Put your toy town away," Edna said. "If you're going to get sidelined by a cat's mind games, you'll miss the big picture."

"Which is what, exactly?"

Edna guided us around the side of the house. "Just look at this place."

Vinnie's big garage was gone now, replaced by the smallest,

cutest red barn I'd ever seen. It was like something out of a children's picture book. The trim white fence that surrounded it was only five feet high. That was great for peering inside at a fluffy white sheep and an equally pristine pygmy goat.

"I've never seen a sheep that white," I said. "Where did they find it?"

"They didn't find it, they made it," Edna said. "It's spray-painted, like they do at agricultural fairs. The goat, too."

"Seriously? They spray-painted the livestock?"

"I doubt the network wants dirt and mud intruding on their vision of quaint country life. All is sweet and picture-perfect here."

"It won't stay that way for long," I said. "One thing you can count on with animals is dung. If they're fed, they poop. The farmer's cycle of life."

A man who looked to be nearly 70 came out of the barn wearing overalls and a Stetson. He looked a lot like Charlie, my silver fox farm manager. Except that Charlie never carried a dustpan on a long pole, along with a broom and a small shovel.

"I'm guessing his job is to make sure poop never hits the snow," Jilly said, laughing.

I leaned over the fence. "You're right. This snow is pristine. That's impossible."

Evie Springdale came up behind us, red curls exploding under a green wool hat. "Nothing's impossible in the film world, Ivy. There's a snow machine behind the barn. They freshen it up on the hour."

Taking off my own hat, I rubbed my forehead. This whole scene —and it was a scene— was giving me a headache. "Why would anyone want to watch a reality show about a farm that whitewashes reality?"

"Are you really asking me that?" Evie said. "For every follower you have who wants to see the real thing, there are fifty who want perfection. Faraway Farm is going to deliver them that."

"Wow. I don't even know what to say, except that my worries about this show mirroring my own life were unfounded. There's no whitewashing my manure pile."

"Wait till you see what's going on inside," Evie said. "Vivian is baking a perfect pie."

"Baking for real?" Jilly asked.

Evie laughed. "Hot out of the oven at Mandy's Country Store. Baked to Vivian's specifications, apparently."

"Let's go home," Jilly said, tugging the sleeve on my parka. "I feel a little sick."

"Not till we see the dog," I said.

"What dog?" she asked.

"Fake Keats. Vivian said the producer got the wrong breed and I'm wondering if they subbed in a new actor dog."

As if on cue, a huge fluffy black and white dog ambled out of the barn and joined the farm assistant. The man rested his hand on the tall dog's head and it gave a swish of its tail.

"What breed is that?" Evie asked. "I've never seen it before."

"I think it's a Caucasian shepherd," I said. "A livestock guardian instead of a herder. Some are nearly two hundred pounds. They're mild mannered, but they'll fight a predator to the death to protect their charges."

The big dog glanced over at Keats and lifted its muzzle. Keats mumbled something that sounded polite. Respectful. Each working dog had a role and there was no competition. The Caucasian shepherd strolled over to let me pat its head and the farm assistant tipped his Stetson. Then the goat tackled the dog from behind and they collapsed into the fake snow.

"Okay, that's adorable," Jilly said, snapping a photo on her phone. "Can we get a big bear like that?"

"Keats, cover your ears," I said. "Jilly's turning traitor. On the bright side, she is encouraging us to get even more animals."

"Only if they come with an assistant."

"And an allowance. Imagine how much that dog would eat."

A group of people came toward us, eating cookies and sipping hot chocolate. Those, at least, smelled real.

"Isn't this remarkable? Such a gorgeous, hospitable place," Heddy Langman said. She was looking at her sister Kaye but I suspected the statement was directed at me. There was no love lost between the Langman sisters and me, since I kept putting their names forward as murder suspects.

"Gorgeous," echoed Beverly Roxton, wife of the town's small animal veterinarian. There was no love lost between us, either, and for the same reason. "I cannot wait to watch this show. The first episode airs tomorrow."

"We're having a watch party," said Laurene Pedal, of Pages and Pastries.

I wasn't sure where I stood with Laurene, having also put *her* name forward to Kellan as a potential killer. Looking at the next group coming toward us, I realized that while I had made many wonderful new friends here, I probably had just as many enemies.

Keats thought so, too. His disliking for the Langmans and Beverly Roxton hadn't abated one bit. They were on our watch list for life.

"Ivy!" The shout came from Teri Mason, who was standing beside the porch with Mabel Halliday. Mabel owned the ceramics store, Miniature Mutts, and our friendship had survived my suspicions of her. I hoped she didn't even know I thought she might be capable of murder. It wasn't personal. Most people were probably capable of murder in the right circumstances. More like the wrong circumstances. Even me. There was no doubt in my mind that I could and would dispatch someone who threatened the lives of my animals. "You need to come inside," Teri called. "There's an urgent matter."

"What could be so urgent?" I muttered.

"Your mother," Kaye Langman said, smiling. Had her teeth always been that pointy? Or had I just never really seen her smile before? "Dahlia's being... well, Dahlia."

That was enough to get my feet moving, and Jilly was a step or two ahead of me. Keats waved his tail merrily as he led the way up the stairs and in the front door.

Inside, so many people milled around that I couldn't see my petite mother. But I could certainly hear her. She was unleashing on someone. I could only hope it wasn't on camera. With the bright, hot lights overhead, I suspected *everything* was on camera.

"Find Mom and herd her back," I told Keats. "Use your teeth if you must."

He set off, deftly weaving through a sea of legs. There was a sudden high-pitched yip that didn't come from the dog.

"Stop that right now, you cur," Mom bellowed. "Ivy Rose Galloway!"

The crowds parted to let us through and we walked onto the kitchen set.

Jilly gasped. "Oh my goodness. It's modeled on ours."

"Only even nicer," I whispered. "Someone had eyes on us, Jilly."

A woman standing at the granite counter was greeting people warmly and handing out cups of steaming hot chocolate. She was wearing overalls and her hair was in a sloppy ponytail. Looking over at us, she gave a tight little smile. Her expression was bland and her hazel eyes serious.

It took me a second to realize I was looking at Vivian Crane. It took me a second longer to realize I was staring into a mirror—or at least a magic mirror that showed what I'd look like in middle age.

"Oh my gosh, she's wearing a wig and contact lenses," I whispered. "Just to look more like me."

Edna snorted behind me. "No wonder Dahlia's having a conniption."

Mom pushed through the crowd, or more specifically, was

pushed by a whirling dervish of a sheepdog, who managed to press people back while urging his sheep forward.

"We really do need one of those," someone said. I turned to see Becky Bower, with Ray and Eric on either side, with their cameras.

"My mother?" I said. "There's one available if you need her. I might even pay you."

"We *do* need a mom," she said, as if the idea had just occurred to her. "But I meant the dog. He's quite talented, whereas Byron just sits there like a blob while the goat climbs all over him."

"Byron? As in Lord Byron, the decadent poet?" I asked.

"I was hoping he'd have more personality when I named him," she said.

"He's doing his job as a livestock guardian," I said. "Make no mistake, he'd move plenty fast if a coyote went after the sheep or goat. There are predators around here."

"So I've heard. At least of the human variety." Becky waggled her eyebrows. "Your dog would be a better bet in a duel to the death."

Keats mumbled a humblebrag. Jilly, Edna and even Mom laughed. Becky tilted her head, missing the joke. Keats-speak was lost on her.

"He's an amazing dog," I said. "And no, he's not for hire. He's got a full-time gig at our place—a real working farm where I muck out the stalls and Jilly peels the potatoes. We don't have a snow machine to—"

"Cut," Becky said. "Ivy, look. We're doing our best to work *with* you, not against you."

"What's that supposed to mean?" I asked. "Why would you work against me?"

Jilly squeezed my elbow as a reminder to lock in my HR persona. I did, but Mom wasn't as easily managed. She straightened her shoulders, threw back her head and claimed more than her share of the space.

"These people want you to keep quiet about what they're doing," Mom said. "About how they're stealing your life story. It's tacky and utterly shameless."

"It's not like that," Becky said. "We're just doing a show here. But we really do want you on the payroll as an advisor, Ivy. We want to do this right, and we don't want bad publicity. No matter what you do, people seem to like you."

There were whispers behind me.

"Why is it always about Ivy? What makes her so interesting?"

"I don't know, but she's all anyone talks about."

"The Galloways are attention seekers. They don't even care who dies."

"I wonder who will play Kellan Harper. I bet he dumps her over this. It's the last straw."

I turned quickly to catch the last speaker. It was Beverly Roxton.

Jilly squeezed my arm again and whispered, "He won't. Don't let her get to you."

It got to me. The other comments rolled off my armor like raindrops but that one sliced through. I was always worried about the last straw with Kellan. Would I know it when I saw it?

Turning back to Becky, I saw the green camera light was on again. I pulled out my best HR smile—the one Vivian was wearing. I was grateful for the armor I'd developed over years of sheer misery in the corporate world.

"Becky, I wish you nothing but the best with your show," I said. "I'm afraid I can't help you in any way, though. I have a contract with the former owner about publicity."

"Hannah Pemberton?" she blurted. "The billionaire?"

"The Pembertons, yes. They're so protective of Runaway Farm's reputation. I'm sure your network's thought all that through."

Her eyes narrowed. "Is that a threat? Because we have a very robust legal team."

"That must be such a comfort," Edna said. Turning to me she

added, "People like them will go down first, you know. In the apocalypse."

I had to fight back a snicker as I held out my hand to Becky. "Look, we got off on the wrong foot. I truly do wish you well. Especially Vivian. It isn't easy to run a farm or even act like it."

It looked like Becky would refuse my hand but someone cleared her throat behind us.

"That's kind of you, Ivy," Vivian said. "You're welcome here at Faraway Farm anytime."

Up close, she looked older than Mom, or at least very tired. The other day in the salon she'd been more feisty. Now she took my hand and shook it.

"Thank you," I said. "I've got to get home and put fifty animals to bed."

"Fifty?" Vivian's shudder gave her away, but Keats had already told me she wasn't an animal lover. Both women got a flat "no" in the character department. "You're as brave as everyone says, Ivy." She glanced toward the door. "There's the mayor. You'll need to stay."

She spoke like someone who was used to issuing orders and having them obeyed. But I still had my free will and a brilliant dog. "Out, buddy. Evasive measures, please."

I didn't need to ask him twice. He was done with this crowd and eager to get home. It was a circuitous route, but I followed the white tuft of his tail that had never led me astray. Jilly clutched my sleeve with one hand and Mom with the other, while Edna brought up the rear.

"I wanted to speak to the mayor," Mom said, once we were outside. "What is this town coming to? That's all I can say."

"Yep, that's all you can say... today." We closed ranks to get her to the truck. Edna slipped into the back seat with Jilly, leaving me to boost Mom into the front.

"Asher has a step for me in his truck," she said, as I shoved her from the rear.

"Stop fighting," I said. "It was easier getting an alpaca in here than you."

"And the miniature horse," Edna said. "They just don't bend like you hope."

"Don't make me laugh," I said, finally getting Mom seated.

"I'm staying with you tonight," she said. "I'm too upset to be alone."

Lately, she was finding more and more excuses to stay at the inn, and worse, she'd upgraded herself to one of the nicer rooms. When I had a full house, that would have to end.

We dropped Edna at her house and drove the rest of the way in silence—if you didn't count Mom's huffy snorts.

I left her in Jilly's custody and went right through the barn to the manure pile, barely scanning the animals as I passed. It was late afternoon, and we'd have to bring the outside animals inside soon. I just needed a few minutes with my shovel and some hard labor to take the edge off. Keats followed me, making an odd squeaking sound that was new to his communications repertoire. It was an alarm of some kind and it stopped me in my tracks.

"What's wrong?" I asked. "Everything looks okay to me."

He panted a quick no-no-no and passed in front of me, tail straight and puffed. A bad omen if ever there was one.

"Trouble in the henhouse?" I asked.

The triple "no" pant came again as he emerged into the cold, his breath steaming out behind him like a banner.

"What then?" My visions of a good dung-bashing were fading fast. "Drama Llama and the thugs?" The donkeys and camelids normally didn't come in unless it was brutally cold. Charlie had built them a shelter, which they dismissed as being for sissies and banged up with kicking. Keats' squeals got louder as I racked my brains. "The only one left is..."

Yes-yes-yes. The pant came faster and the steam drifted away from the bristling dog.

"Wilma," I said.

Keats went into a point at the empty pig pen. She was gone.

CHAPTER SIX

"No-no-no," I panted, running around the perimeter of Wilma's pasture with Keats. "She can't have escaped. We've done everything but build a fortress around Mount Wilma. We had her beat."

The sly sow had escaped before, on both my watch and Hannah's. She was a freewheeler who liked to explore both field and forest. A wallow in the fetid swamp on Edna's property was her favorite fair-weather destination. She'd almost drowned me there once.

"How did she get out?" I called after Keats. "Show me."

There was no reason to ask. He was already leading me to the spot where two slats in a very sturdy fence sat slightly ajar. It was as far from the barn as possible and completely out of sight from the house.

She was a smart pig, but she wasn't *that* smart, at least in my estimation. I flattered myself that I knew her fairly well by now.

Wilma obviously had an accomplice with prehensile thumbs and enough sense to stay out of sight lines. Pulling out my phone, I texted Edna and then Jilly. My gloved thumb hovered over the next number. Was it worth the lecture?

Of course it was. My pig was running loose on what would be a very cold winter's night. I needed all the backup I could get. Pressing speaker, I started back to the barn to get my gear.

"What?" The voice on the other end was even more clipped than usual.

"Hi to you, too," I said.

"This had better be important," Cori Hogan said. "I'm with a client."

She was a respected and popular dog trainer in Dorset Hills, despite being nearly constantly available to help animals. Figured I'd catch her on the one day she was actually busy.

"I'd text if it weren't important," I said.

"Good idea," she said. "Hang up and text."

"Only it *is* important, Cori. Do I ever call you just to shoot the breeze?"

"I don't shoot the breeze. And this is no time to start." I could sense her black-gloved hand, with its orange middle finger, was gesticulating. When she was that intense, the fingers flew. "Maybe I just don't want to deal with whatever you're calling about right now. It's always bad news."

That was true. There was no one other than Kellan I talked to on the phone regularly, come to think of it. With Jilly in the house, I was covered for anything else. That meant my calls did mean trouble and people would start avoiding them eventually.

"Well? Is it bad news?" Cori continued. "Tell me I'm wrong. Please. I might even apologize. Although I wouldn't count on it."

I was inside the barn now, gathering what I thought I might need for the search. "You're not wrong."

"Try it in the affirmative. It sounds so much better." She was brightening now, warming to whatever challenge lay ahead. "I'll be more likely to help you out of whatever bind you're in."

"I said you're right. I only call when I'm in trouble and I'm sorry about that. I promise to touch base now and then, just to see how you're doing between emergencies, if you'll gather the troops and come out right now. The more, the better, because she's got a good head start. At least there are tracks."

I set the phone on top of a post and wriggled into Charlie's heavy fleece-lined overalls. I didn't have time to go up to the house and get my own. On the plus side, I didn't even need to take off my boots. On the negative, I wouldn't be able to maneuver as well with the extra fabric. Wilma could outrun me at the best of times.

Cori sighed. "Spit it out or put Keats on the line."

"Let me ask you this. Of all the animals, which would you least like to hunt down?"

"Wilma," she said without hesitation. "Because she's smarter than the average sow and twice as mean." There was a pause. "Tell me it's not Wilma."

"Then I'd be lying. Because she's gone. And worse, someone set her free."

"Not again. It seems like just yesterday I was tracking her through the bush with Hannah. It was warmer then."

"At least the swamp's frozen," I said. "At least I think so. I haven't had reason to check. That's the first place I'll go."

"Don't go anywhere," Cori said. "We only have a few hours till dark so we need to deploy with military precision. I've already sent out the 911. I'll swing home to get Clem, and Remi can bring Leo. She's spoiled him for regular work but he does have the beagle nose."

"Edna's on her way and Jilly's trying my family. Somehow they're always conveniently unavailable when there's an animal crisis. Asher and Kellan are on evening shift."

"Just as well," Cori said, calling goodbye to her client and then raising her voice as the engine of her truck turned over. "Kellan hates taking orders from me as much as I love giving them."

I laughed. "There can only be one commander in chief and when it comes to rescue, you get the badge."

"Flattery is usually wasted on me but in this case, I'll take it," Cori said. "Is that Edna's ATV roaring up?"

"Yep. I only left her half an hour ago but she's already in fatigues."

"We can only hope to be as cool as she is by eighty," Cori said.

Having surrendered me into Edna's capable hands, Cori hung up without a goodbye. I explained what I'd found while I trapped Keats and wrestled him into his coat. Make that one of his coats. I had a few now in strategic locations, ready to ambush him when the need arose. Despite a winter of unrelenting cold, he continued to turn into a spineless deadweight at the mere sight of a jacket. Sometimes he threw in trembling and whining for dramatic effect.

"Get it together, fearsome fur hero," I grunted, trying to connect the Velcro as he recovered muscle tone and started squirming. "This is a job for superdog, but in all the stories, he's wearing a down coat."

"I'm glad you're taking this so well," Edna said. "It's like sabotage is all in a day's work for you now."

"Hardly. But rounding up all the livestock at Vinnie's was tougher than this, right?"

Her frown said otherwise. "I can't rope that pig and I did try the day she was in my garden."

"There are tracks. You can circle out front on the ATV and the dogs will work with you to herd her back. I'm sure she won't go far in this cold."

Edna drew down her eyebrows to add to the frown. "Wilma's finally found some fool to set her free and she's not going to blow a chance like this."

"Who would set her free?" I asked. "And better yet, why?"

Now the eyebrows and the frown got a little help from rolling eyes. "You're about as smart as Wilma so I'm sure you can hazard a guess. Who just threatened you?"

"Becky Bower? Why would she do that?"

"I doubt she did it herself. She couldn't have been in two places at once. But I'm guessing one of the crew managed to slip away while we were over there and made a statement you'd understand back here."

"And the statement is what? That I should back their stupid copycat show?"

"Something like that."

Jilly walked into the barn in heavy winter clothes that still managed to look polished, except for the bag over her shoulder that contained the ever-stylish marmalade cat.

"They wouldn't take it that far, would they?" Jilly asked. "You can't be that big a threat to their production."

"Becky seemed very concerned about Ivy's supposed likability. I guess she's got the 'it' factor," Edna said, shaking her head. Her perm was completely hidden by her heaviest weight camo hat with fleecy earmuffs. "There's no accounting for taste."

"That's crazy. As if I could compete with Vivian Crane, a star in the reality space." I shook my head, too. "After being the grim reaper of HR, it's impossible to imagine a world where I've got any 'it.'"

"You've got something all right," Edna said. "Look no further than Chief Hotstuff for confirmation."

Keats mumbled something that sounded indignant.

"Exactly, buddy," I said. "The only thing remarkable about me is my dog. Keats has the 'it' factor."

"They know that, too. Poor Byron is sloppy seconds," Jilly said. "Becky's likely pounding the virtual pavement looking for Keats' twin right now."

"Good luck with that," I said. "There's no match in this universe."

His next mumble didn't even strive to be humble.

"If they tried to undermine you by setting Wilma free, it'll backfire," Jilly said. "Especially if we can find proof. Asher's coming out to look for evidence."

"He won't find much," I said, pulling out my phone to show

them the pictures. "They raked over human prints and then hopped onto an ATV. From what little I could see, they drove toward the highway." I enlarged one photo. "This one's good though. See that crushed bush? It looks like someone went down hard, very likely with a pig on top of them. Her prints are all over and they couldn't fully rake their embarrassment away."

"Let the cops deal with that," Jilly said. "We'll find Wilma, and if this is about Faraway Fake Farm, it will blow over as soon as they realize you're no threat to ratings."

I sighed. "I never thought I'd say this, but I wish I'd taken Evie up on her offer."

"Too late, yet never too late," another voice said. It was Evie, walking into the barn with a big Rescue Mafia contingent. There were familiar faces—Cori, Bridget and Remi—and many I hadn't met before. I'd had plenty of animal emergencies, but apparently this ranked higher than the others. They probably all knew Wilma and what she was capable of doing.

"Do you really think it's them?" Jilly asked. "It's one thing to talk smack about Ivy and another to put her animals in jeopardy."

"I wouldn't put it past any reality show to do just that," Evie said. "It's just like politics. Discrediting you and your standard of care would benefit them."

"Right," I said. "People will latch onto the message that I can't keep my pig home and safe, whereas all is fresh and whitewashed for Vivian at Faraway Farm."

"Sounds about right," Cori said, directing us all out into the driveway with much flashing of orange fingers. "Hannah went through exactly the same thing when our former mayor targeted her."

"Evie, you countered that with The Princess and the Pig," Remi said, setting Leo's four white paws on the snow-covered gravel. Normally she clutched him like a baby in tense moments, but he was needed on active duty. "Can't you do it again?"

"They've got more firepower. Vivian Crane has a following and while she might not know much about farming, she has plenty of creds in entertaining and food."

"I hate to say it but I liked her Cupcake Millionaire show," Remi said.

Cori held a finger to her lips. The orange one. "Leave the cupcake talk till the pig is safe."

"And others are safe from the pig," Evie added. "That would be exactly the kind of story that would get us in trouble. If Wilma was... well, Wilma."

"I think Wilma gets a bad rap," Remi said. "I was there the day Hannah rescued her. This pig was neglected, abused and overbred. It's no wonder she's a little cranky."

Remorse swirled through me like black smoke. I'd never been as fond of Wilma as many of the other animals, especially Alvina the alpaca, and now Bocelli and Clippers. That was mainly because Wilma had almost killed me. She also frequently proved that I was batting out of my league as a hobby farmer. Over and over she outsmarted me and even Keats. We couldn't think like a pig. Still, Remi's words reminded me that Wilma was just a rescue animal with a traumatic past. In time she might overcome it, just as I had. At least, mostly.

We spread out in what I'd come to know as typical rescue formation: a long horizontal line, walking a few yards apart. That way we couldn't miss anything.

Normally we moved slowly and steadily but today we had prints and dogs with good noses. We had to move fast before the scent and prints faded with fresh snow, not to mention darkness closing in. The days were supposedly getting longer now but it sure didn't feel like it.

The walking was hard and hazardous with the crusty white blanket concealing logs and, it eventually turned out, bogs. A soaker flooded my boot not far from what I called the pig pool near Edna's lane.

"Why isn't this frozen?" I asked, hopping as I emptied my boot. "Is it a magical pig bog?"

"There's a deep underground creek," Edna said. "Moving water doesn't usually freeze. And we've had a few thaws."

"She was here," Cori said, kneeling. "Poked around by the looks of things and thought better of it."

We moved on.

And moved on.

The bush all started to look the same. No one else seemed to flag but me, so I attributed it to my wet foot, which felt like it was packed in ice. I thought about the most recent murder victim, who'd been discovered in a similar situation, and shuddered.

Keats circled back and touched my glove with his nose. "It's okay. Thank you, though."

"Lock it down, Ivy," Cori called to me. "The dog can't work at peak capacity if he's worried about your delicate feelings."

Jilly reached out and squeezed my arm as Keats returned to lead the pack. His tail was up and his ears forward. At least someone was having a good time.

"We'll get through this together," she said. "Just as we have everything else."

Edna was on my other side, having found the terrain too treacherous for the ATV. She delivered a "buck up" punch to my shoulder. "Look on the bright side. It's not a murder."

"True," I said. "Isn't it strange when the absence of murder needs to be noted?"

"Unlike many, I see the upside in those murders," Edna said. "We've become uniquely qualified to deal with what's coming."

"In the zombie apocalypse?" Jilly asked, smiling.

"Any kind of apocalypse, natural or otherwise. Outside the military, it's normally difficult to get boots-on-the-ground training."

"Hello!" Cori's voice was a verbal slap with a glove. "This isn't a tea party. If that pig is in earshot, she's running in the other direction."

"She must be ready to come home," I said, hoping my quaver came off as cold instead of fear. "It's freezing, and nearly dark."

"That won't bother Wilma," Cori said. "She'd take freedom over a cushy stall any day. Why do you think she prefers to be outside all the time?"

I sighed. "Because she's been training for this moment."

Cori laughed. "Maybe. The point is, she'll be fine. She's got a good coat of fur and about a hundred extra pounds on her."

"Wilma is not overweight," I said. "She's perfectly proportioned... for a pig."

"Oh, she's fat all right," Edna said. "You keep trying to buy her love with food. That never works, with animals or children."

"Ouch." I rarely took offense at Edna's comments but I was sensitive at the moment and Keats couldn't take the edge off for me.

Edna shrugged. "I call it like I see it."

I was almost miserable enough to comment on her record of terrorizing children in the school vaccination program, but reminded myself that she was doing the best she could at the time. Maybe I could give myself the same grace. But not till this was over.

"I'm glad Wilma is pleasantly plump," Jilly said. "That will help if she's on the loose for a bit."

"She'll find shelter eventually," Cori said. "The only problem is that this pig can cover a lot of ground. She's surprisingly agile for an overfed—"

"Never mind," I said. "What about predators?"

"The only risk is coyotes—and it would take a pack of them, considering her size. I'm not too worried about that."

"It's the human predators we need to worry about," Evie called from further down the line.

Horror ran through me like an underground creek. "You think someone would hunt my poor pig?"

"In an apocalypse, maybe," Edna said. "No one else hunts around here, and even I gave that up. Social stigma."

"I meant human predators who dine on gossip and reputations," Evie said. "You could be the trophy on their walls if we don't find Wilma quickly."

Cori raised her glove and all I could see in the fading light was the orange flare. "We've got to call it a night. It won't do Wilma—or any of the animals we help—any good if we fall or freeze. Let's regroup tomorrow."

"Come back to the inn for dinner, at least," Jilly said. "It may not be cupcakes, but I can throw something together."

"Vivian seemed nice in that show," Remi said. "I guess it's hard to be tough around cupcakes."

"The season premiere of Faraway Farm is tonight," Evie said. "They shot most of it in a studio in Boston."

"Should be good for a laugh," Cori said, turning the troops.

"Or a clue as to our next steps," Evie said, arms flailing as she slid across a small pond. "We've got to handle these people carefully. One wrong move and tensions could escalate."

Shivering, I reached automatically for Keats' ears. To my surprise, they were ready and waiting. He'd given up one job for another.

"I left the corporate world behind for a reason," I said. "I couldn't handle the cutthroat politics anymore. There was no 'human' in human relations."

Evie, on the other hand, had a spring in her step. She may have left politics behind but she still enjoyed strategy.

"We'll figure it out," she said, sliding on the ice deliberately this time. "Let the games begin."

CHAPTER SEVEN

I fully expected Faraway Farm, the TV show, to be hilarious—in the bad way. Nearly 20 of us gathered in the family room to watch, eating the delicious pasta dish Jilly seemingly pulled out of thin air. As the show went on, however, forks slowed and animated conversation stalled. By the time the credits rolled, we all stared at each other baffled, or in my case, furious. How dare they take my life and do it better? Make it simple and easy and downright elegant in places? I'd never had an elegant moment since my boots landed on this farm's soil.

"Well," Remi said. "That wasn't terrible."

"It wasn't great, either," Evie said. "Felt forced to me. It's quite a stretch to believe Vivian Crane tended the chickens that set her up for that frittata. Although I admit I'll probably visit their website to download the recipe."

"I'm sure it was rubbery," I told Jilly. "It looked overcooked to me."

Jilly laughed. "My vanity will survive the fact that they rolled us together into one person. We're practically twins anyway."

"It's a shame she modeled her style after Ivy instead of you,

Jilly," Mom said. "Those overalls looked dreadful. And that hair! Even Ivy doesn't do pigtails."

"Maybe I should," I said. "Stencil on a few freckles and learn to square dance."

Mom smoothed her red dress, which was different from the one she'd worn earlier. Had she moved her entire wardrobe here, too?

"Still not funny, darling. But I know you're stressed about your pig."

"Not to mention identity theft," Edna said. "It's a total invasion of your privacy."

"Preppers might be next," I said. "Is that in the zeitgeist, too, Evie?"

She shook her head. "Hits too close to home. People are worried about the state of the world. They long for the days when a rooster crowed us awake."

"I bet there's no rooster at Faraway Farm," I said. "Aladdin is loud and annoying. I bet they don't even know how many tons of poop chickens produce a year. Their manure will never be properly managed."

"Maybe they'll let you guest star with your manure management pro tips," Edna said, smirking. "It's a real issue for homesteaders. People complain about it all the time."

"Maybe there's no poop at Faraway Farm," I said. "If there's any justice in the world, though, Vivian will pass out from the fumes and do a face plant in dung, just like I did. Or maybe there will be a small explosion. Nothing big enough to harm the animals, of course."

"All five of them," Cori said, rolling her eyes. "As if two chickens produced enough eggs for that fancy brunch. They're not even laying right now."

"The horse, sheep, goat and chickens are all white," I said. "Will viewers believe they stay that way naturally? And if she thinks that goat is going to stay in that dinky pen she's got a rude awakening coming. A bored goat is trouble."

"Maybe you *should* be a consultant," Edna said. "Infiltrate from the inside and look for weaknesses to exploit."

"That's not a bad idea," Mom said. "Perhaps she'd take some good advice from me about the overalls."

I shook my head. "All I care about is finding Wilma and going about my regular business."

Remi tried to offer me Leo, who was lolling in her arms again after trailing Wilma valiantly like a regular hound. Keats, who was leaning against my leg, gave a grumble loud enough to startle her. He wasn't arm candy but he provided his own excellent brand of therapy.

"Sorry, Keats," she said, backing away. "I don't know what I was thinking."

"You were just picking up on my worries and being generous with your dog," I said. "I appreciate it, but I'll be fine. A good night's sleep and I'll be back in the field tomorrow."

Cori gave the signal to decamp and the women rose almost as one and went to the front hall. That's when the tiny trainer lost control of the troops, however. While she stood outside on the porch with her gloved hands shoved in her pockets, everyone started hugging each other as if the apocalypse loomed. Normally I wasn't a fan of such flagrant affection, but tonight I took all the hugs I could get. When I missed a few people, Keats herded me around and gave me a pointed shove with his muzzle. He wasn't a fan of flagrant affection either, but he knew a good thing when he saw it.

"Would you just stop?" Cori said. "Before Edna and I turn into human popsicles?"

The women surged through the door and staged a group hug on both of them.

I expected Edna to put up a fight, but other than shielding her perm she succumbed to the wave of goodwill.

"Reconvene here at ten," Cori said, disengaging herself and running down the stairs ahead of the others. "We need the light."

KEATS, Percy and I were on the road before eight the next morning. My errand wouldn't take long and I'd be back in plenty of time to greet the Rescue Mafia and resume our search for Wilma.

"This is probably a bad idea," I said, taking the slow route through town. The back roads were faster but I still had flashbacks from our very bumpy ride in a blizzard on Christmas Eve with Edna at the wheel.

Keats mumbled something noncommittal. No matter how it turned out, he was happy to be going on a secret mission I didn't even mention to Jilly. Percy was curled up beside him in the passenger seat trying to catch a little more beauty sleep. The cat was totally comfortable in his little parka, unlike Keats, who tore at his coat with his teeth when he got the chance. Mom kept stitching them up. One she'd pulled apart entirely to make him an original Dahlia production. The odds were against his liking it, but I wouldn't complain if she went back to her apartment to spend some quality time with her sewing machine.

Keats gave me a look with his eerie blue eye.

"What? I love Mom but that doesn't mean I want to live with her. What if she starts bringing her boyfriends home?" How she kept such a robust stable of eligible men in an area where women had a hard time meeting the right guy was beyond me. "Do you know she wants to teach rotational dating 101? Tell me that wouldn't be awkward."

He turned back to stare at the road. Mom usually got a free pass with him, no matter how much trouble she caused.

"You're right. I shouldn't let myself get sidetracked. This is going to take my full focus. I'm bringing all my HR expertise to bear." I turned down the long lane. "I hope I still got it. I'm not the woman I used to be, buddy. For better or worse."

He turned and warmed me to the core with his brown eye and a wide smile. No matter who I'd become, he was my biggest fan. Bigger even than Kellan.

The rumble in his throat said, "You'd better believe it."

We drove under the black arch that read "Faraway Far" with the "m" hanging by a thread. It wasn't made of rusted-out iron like mine, but it was a decent reproduction.

I wasn't sure what to expect. Did they actually live here when they were shooting in town, or stay at a hotel and drive to the farm set?

There were several cars in the parking area. One Mercedes and a few that looked like rentals. The proof of the falseness of it all was that there wasn't a single pickup truck. No farm in Clover Grove could manage without one.

"I'd like to see Vivian drive a pickup with a standard transmission," I said. "See how real that gets."

Keats mumbled something calming. If I got myself riled, I'd lose my advantage.

Not that I really had an advantage.

"All I want is to make peace. I used to be a skilled negotiator, you know." I pulled up beside the Mercedes and switched off the ignition. "You *do* know. Because I've had to negotiate with a few people not to kill us." That made me smile. "Clearly I haven't lost my chops because we're still here."

He gave me a happy pant and I smoothed my hair. It had been tempting to wear it in pigtails but that would just be poking the bear. No poking the bear when you need to save a pig.

"How do I look? I wore my best jeans and a nice sweater so they'd take me seriously. I'll have to change back into farmer Ivy before anyone sees me later."

He placed both white paws on my leg and then pumped a few times. The gesture always meant "go."

"Fine. I'm stalling and I admit it. I feel like I should have an agent with me."

I opened the door and released Keats. Percy unwound himself, yawned and then mewed.

"I don't know," I said. "I didn't see a cat. They really should have one. Maybe your friend Snowflake could get some day work. Roles for a white cat are hard to find."

Keats mumbled something from the driveway. *Stalling.*

I slid down from the truck and Percy leapt from the seat onto my shoulder. No reason to get his paws wet when he could catch a ride.

Becky opened the door on my second knock. They must have seen me coming because the green light on Ray's camera was on.

"Good morning," I said, dialing my smile past neutral to sweet. "I'm here to see a lady about a pig."

"A pig?" Becky said. "We don't have a pig at Faraway Farm. Yet."

For the first time I wondered if they'd been trying to steal Wilma, rather than just set her free. There was no doubt in my mind that she'd have put up a fight. That might explain the crushed bush. Maybe someone tried to leash the nice piggy.

"No? That's probably for the best," I said. "Wilma's a feisty one. Mind you all my animals are rescues who had hard lives."

"Yes?" Becky's guard was up. I'd have to initiate maneuvers.

"It was nice to see such happy animals in your little barn. And Byron seems like an absolute doll. Keats took to him right away."

Becky crossed her arms. "What's up, Ivy? Yesterday you wouldn't give us the time of day."

"Just came to have a quick word with Vivian. I won't keep you long."

"She isn't up yet," Becky said. "We had a party here after the season premiere."

Keats didn't wait for an invitation. He slipped through their feet and then upstairs. "I'll wait for her," I said. "Do I smell coffee?"

"No," Becky said. "You smell our schedule burning as we stand around talking. Time is money in the film business."

"Of course." I sensed she was an unmovable force, so I pushed in front of Ray instead. As I suspected, he didn't hold me back. On the contrary, he let me through and continued shooting while I walked ahead of them into the kitchen. I knew exactly where to find the coffeemaker as it sat in the same place in virtually the same kitchen as mine. It was even the same model, although the production could certainly afford better. "Incredible eye for detail. How did you manage to copy the décor down to the last detail?"

Becky shrugged. "Every nice farmhouse has a kitchen like this."

I laughed. "There's no kitchen like this in Clover Grove as far as I know. Homesteaders are trying to live off the land, even off the grid. Granite is out of their snack bracket for the most part. Mine too, of course. I caught a lucky break with Hannah." Percy kneaded my shoulder and I nodded. "Of course, the website has photos. You're right."

"Who's right?" Becky looked genuinely confused. I was going to end up on their show chitchatting to my cat if I wasn't more careful.

"Sorry. Talking to myself. Guess I spend too much time alone in the barn."

I opened the cupboard where we kept our mugs and was relieved to see they were using it for spices. The next one, where we kept cereal, had the mugs. Becky said nothing as I poured the coffee, took a sip, and then turned to lean against the counter. Percy shifted to get his balance and then started grooming himself.

"Why don't you just cut to the chase?" Becky said.

"I already did. I'm here to talk to Vivian about my pig."

"About your what?" Vivian was standing in the doorway wearing a negligee like nothing I'd ever own. It was pink and had feathered edges and was transparent in spots. Not the dangerous spots, thank goodness.

"My pig," I said. "Good morning."

"It's not that good when a wet nose jabs your eyelid to wake you up." She rubbed her face and I noticed her eyes were blue again. "He let himself into the room." Turning to Becky, she said, "Why isn't Byron that smart? Why isn't Byron Keats?"

That made me smile. The two poets had very little in common as far as I could remember.

"Byron's an outdoor dog," I said. "He'll never be happy in the house poking your eyelid while he has livestock. And if he doesn't have livestock, he'll pine. That's why he's on this earth."

"You're very odd, Ivy," she said. "And I don't think I can pretend otherwise without a coffee." She nudged me aside while glaring at Ray. "Turn that thing off. You know I don't roll camera unless I'm dressed and ready. It's in my contract." Under her breath she added, "Or it will be."

"But we could get some good footage of Ivy talking to her cat," Becky suggested.

"Later." Vivian took out a cup and poured. There was barely any coffee left and she raised her eyebrows at Becky. "Make more coffee while I find out about the pig that brought Ivy crawling back to my door."

So it was *her* door, now. Not the production's. It was hard to know if she was in character or not. Best to assume she was and that any of this footage could be used against me.

I swallowed the rest of my coffee before speaking. "When I got home yesterday, I found that someone had released Wilma, my pig. I searched for hours with my friends but we haven't found her."

"I'm sorry to hear that." Vivian stared at me over the rim of her cup as she sipped the inch of coffee I'd left her. "Is there something we could do to help? That's what happens out here in the country, right? You pitch in for barn raisings and potlucks."

"And square dancing," I said. I couldn't help myself. I thought Keats would laugh but he gave me a look that said zip it. "Just kidding. I'm really here because I realize I should have been more neighborly yesterday. Many of my friends did pitch in to help me search and it reminded me to do better. So I'm here now to offer my support if you still need it."

"Well, Ivy, that's kind of you," Vivian said. "I'm surprised a pig could bring about such a change of heart. She must be very special."

"They all are. Even the ones that try to trample me. I care about them."

My phone buzzed and I pulled it out of my pocket. "I'd better go. There's been a sighting." Keats cocked his head and his ears came forward. "At Gertie's. Isn't that strange? How could she have come so far so fast?"

"Gertie Rhodes?" Vivian said. "Is that the woman whose property joins up with this one? She was just awful to our locations people. We'd hoped to include her but..."

"She didn't fit the profile," I said. "Of the sweet small-town neighbor. Like anywhere else, there are some big personalities here."

I started walking to the front door. "Sorry about Keats poking you in the eye, Vivian. And thanks for hearing me out."

"Hang on," she called after me. I turned and she and Becky were having a silent communication that involved eyebrows and shoulders. "Just give me time to get dressed and we'll help you look for this Wilbur."

"Wilma," I said. "Thanks so much for offering but it's not a great idea. The terrain at Gertie's is quite treacherous. I was back there not long ago to get a Christmas tree."

"And hunt for treasure," Becky said. "Or so we heard."

"Keats did discover a few caches of stolen goods," I said. "It's true."

Vivian glared at Becky. "Byron would never find buried gold. He's a dud."

"Give Byron a chance," I said. "Guardian breeds are steady and unflappable. He's absolutely perfect for his job. Keats is bred for other things."

"Digging for gold?" Becky asked.

"That's just his hobby. He has energy to burn. And he's going to burn some now in deep snow."

"Call wardrobe, Becky," Vivian said, heading for the stairs. "See if they have any snowshoes."

"You'll need a bulletproof vest, judging by what I heard," Becky muttered. "Maybe Ivy's neighbor could hook us up."

"Edna and Gertie are old pals," I said, opening the door. "Cut from the same cloth."

"Thanks for the warning. We'll meet you at Gertie's in fifteen minutes. Don't start without us."

Percy dug in his claws as I walked down the front stairs. He'd never bothered to dismount inside and he launched into the truck when I opened the door. Like most cats, he conserved his energy till it was really needed.

"Boys, it's going to be a day," I said. "Let's try to act normal, okay?"

Keats panted a ha-ha-ha and I joined him.

"Well, let's try not to embarrass Kellan then," I said. "A more achievable goal."

I called Jilly to fill her in and that was my fatal mistake. The passenger door opened and Vivian, now dressed in the coat and ruffled scarf she wore in the salon that first day, flicked her matching purple leather glove to shoo the animals into the back seat. "Get in, Becky," she said, gesturing for her assistant to climb in the back with Keats and Percy. "Use your phone to film as we drive to this Gertie's."

She swung into the passenger seat with such ease that for the first time, I wondered if I'd underestimated her.

CHAPTER EIGHT

Taking the highway to Gertie's place would have been shorter than the twisty rough ride over the snowy trails but now my priorities had changed. I was willing to sacrifice a few minutes for the small pleasure of jolting Vivian and Becky around. I even hit a couple of logs that I could have easily avoided just to hear the sound effects. Keats gave a little whine and Percy an exasperated yowl but as it turned out, I stalled anyway. I turned the key again, got the truck rolling and then stalled a few yards later. My nerves were showing.

"Oh, for heaven's sake, let me drive," Vivian said, as we started moving once more. "My Mercedes is a stick. There's no point having a nice car without handling it yourself."

Keats mumbled something that sounded like a compliment.

Vivian glanced over her shoulder at him and continued. "I wasn't always a star, you know. My granddad was a farmer and I spent summer vacations up to my armpits in corn. This show isn't the stretch you might think."

"I have no opinion either way," I said, impressed that the lie came out sounding HR sanitized. "I just don't want to be in the limelight myself."

Becky kicked the back of my seat. Accidentally, I'm sure. "You seem to end up in the limelight a lot for someone who claims not to like it."

"That's true, unfortunately," I said. "I got a pretty serious concussion after rescuing Keats and haven't fully recovered yet. Might never recover. Sometimes I get myself into situations I wouldn't have before."

"Poor judgment," Vivian said.

"Maybe. Or poor impulse control. When I see something wrong, I want to correct it. Immediately." I gave her a smile. "Jilly's always asking me to count to ten before doing anything risky."

"How far do you normally get?" Vivian said.

"Two," I admitted. "On a good day."

Keats put one white paw on my shoulder and murmured a warning. About what, I wasn't sure. Was there something out here I was missing?

"What's he worried about?" Vivian asked.

"Probably about hitting another log," I said. "Or maybe Wilma."

"You two seem to have a code," she said. "I wish Byron was smart enough to have a code." She straightened her purple scarf. "I've never liked animals, really. Most of them are boring and all of them are dirty."

"I bet you could develop a great relationship with Byron," I said, driving out of the bush about halfway down Gertie's lane. "He's a very smart dog."

"Please. He's a plug and a dud. Every shot he's just lying around with the goat on top of him."

"There's plenty going on under all that fluff." I slowed in the lane to finish my thought. "You folks asked for my insights and I'll share one. Developing a relationship with that dog should be your top priority. It would be good for you, good for the dog, and good for the show."

"For the show? I don't think so," Vivian said. "Reality shows live or die on conflict."

"There are plenty of other ways to find conflict on a farm. I bet your viewers would love to see the sweet side of Byron and the rest of the animals. That's the best thing about farm life for me. I try to form a bond with all of them."

"Didn't work with the pig, did it?" Becky asked.

"Not yet," I said. "Some take longer than others, depending on their past. Or maybe my past."

Vivian touched my sleeve. "How do you propose I develop this connection with Byron?"

"Oh, that'll be easy," I said. "Take over his care. Feed him, walk him, train with him. Above all, just spend time with him."

"He won't come inside," she said. "He gets to the doorway and the brakes come on."

"Yeah, you've got to work *with* his instincts not against them. Go down to his pasture. Get him a few more white goats to look after."

She made a disgusted sound. "I'll be focusing on cooking and entertaining. That's more my thing."

"Well, you're doing yourself and the dog a disservice," I said. "You'll both miss out on something wonderful. He's got the 'it' factor.' I felt it."

Shooting another look over her shoulder at Becky, Vivian said, "Get hold of a dog I can bond with inside. Find my Keats."

I laughed. "Keats doesn't love being inside, either. He's a dog who needs to be doing. And I like to be busy, too. That's why it works. We're up before dawn and don't stop till we drop."

Vivian sighed. "I should have taken the other show they offered. About living large on little. But no, I let Becky talk me into this foolishness."

"It's going to break you out," Becky said. "The network's under-valued you too long."

"You mean it's going to break me," Vivian said. "I don't get paid enough, that's for sure."

I'd called ahead to warn Gertie I was coming, mainly so she'd put something on under her old brown poncho. Happily, she'd found some old sweatpants. Her long gray braid hung over one shoulder, reaching well past her waist. It held your eye—until you noticed the rifle hidden in the folds of her poncho.

"I didn't say you could bring friends, Ivy," she called from the porch as I got out of the truck.

"For starters, they're not friends," I said, as Keats and Percy ran up to greet her. "And I didn't invite them. They offered to help me find my pig."

Gertie laughed. "Our lady of the purple coat is going to trudge through the back forty with you? How much you want to bet you'll be rescuing her, not the pig?"

"Apparently conflict makes for good TV, Gertie. So I suppose if Vivian falls into your swamp, ratings will soar."

"Very funny," Vivian said. "This show is about quaint farm life, not wrestling alligators."

"There are no alligators in Clover Grove," Becky said.

"Untrue," I said. "My brother rescued one that escaped from a collector. Where there's one there's usually more."

"Not funny, Ivy," Vivian said. "Hasn't your mother told you you're not funny?"

"She sure has, but I keep on believing." I grinned at Gertie. "Anyway, 'gators hibernate so we're safe from that particular threat today. But there are so many more."

"Yeah. Like me," Gertie said. "I told you TV people that I want nothing to do with you. I told you to stay off my property, or else. Yet here you are, using Ivy to get to me."

"It's only because of the pig sighting," I said. "I wouldn't have come otherwise, I promise."

"Did the report come from a reputable source?" she asked.

"Because few people dare to come out this way now, what with the cops helping me chase off trespassers."

I pulled out my phone and studied it. "It's just from the town's website."

Gertie flung back her braid in disgust. "Ivy, you've been played. The TV show is behind this so-called sighting. It's a hoax to get us involved."

"That's not true," Vivian said. "You can be sure I'd have dressed for the wilds if I'd been part of this decision. And I do have veto power."

"We have wardrobe coming," Becky told her. "They'll be here any minute."

"I'm not waiting for you," I said. "If Wilma's out there, I want to find her."

"And if Ivy's not with you, you're not going," Gertie said. "I don't want you roaming on my property unsupervised."

"I'll go ahead with Ivy," Vivian said. "We'll stay in touch by phone and you and the crew can catch up."

"Great, let's go," I said, beckoning to Keats and Percy. I trudged away quickly, hoping Vivian would flounder in city boots that weren't designed for hiking through bush.

She kept up better than I expected. In fact, she only took one header on a slick patch, whereas I took three in my expedition-style boots.

"How exactly are we going to find this pig?" she asked, after about a half mile that felt far longer.

"Keats, primarily," I said. "For a sheepdog, he has a good sniffer. If we find tracks, we'll know the sighting was legit."

"I didn't engineer that report," she said.

"No? You'll excuse me for doubting because you were pretty quick to jump onto this mission."

"Recognizing an opportunity isn't the same as creating a fake one," she said. "Besides, if I'd planned it, the camera would be here.

All I've got now is my phone."

"Let's just find the pig if we can."

After a few minutes she added, "This is also an opportunity to get to know each other. I'm interested to know what makes you tick."

What ticked was my internal safe as I locked myself down. While her phone was aimed in my direction she'd get precious little access.

"Here's the thing," I said. "Wilma wants to be on the lam, even in the cold. She won't be hungry enough yet to wave the white flag. So if she hears us or smells us she'll go in the opposite direction."

"How exactly do you plan to corral her then?"

"Keats, of course. Percy will help, too. The cat's a wild card, but also ingenious."

"But you said Wilma's vicious."

I turned quickly. "I most certainly did not. Did someone else tell you she's vicious?"

"Becky, I suppose. She does her homework."

"Well, if the pig's under attack she'll take appropriate action, no question. I'm warning you now, in case we find her."

"Duly noted. I'll take appropriate action, too. Just so you know."

"Let's stay quiet," I said. "The others will join us before long and there will be no hope of surprising Wilma."

There was no trail, so we picked our way over logs and rocks following Keats and Percy, who kept ranging ahead and circling back impatiently. There was something out here, I was sure of it. The dog's ruff rose and settled, rose and settled again, and his ears twitched continuously. For all I knew it could have been a fox or coyote. He'd want to protect me from wildlife.

Finally he went into a point. He froze in position, one paw lifting over unblemished snow. His eyes stared straight ahead into thick bush. Then his tail stood straight out and puffed.

"What's wrong?" Vivian asked. There was a note of alarm in her voice that was either real or very good acting.

"I don't know. Something has him spooked. When he does this it rarely ends well, Vivian." I turned and held up one glove. "Stay here while I investigate with him."

"I will not," she said. "What if whatever it is comes after me?"

"Whether it's Wilma or another predator, it's far more likely to come after the dog or cat, unfortunately." I covered my mouth. "I didn't mean it that way. It's just that they're small and vulnerable."

Percy took his cue and jumped onto my shoulder.

"I'm coming," Vivian said.

"You're not. Stop running down your phone battery by filming me and give Becky a call."

"How long will this take?" she asked.

"Not long. I'll be back soon." I took her phone number and started pushing into the thorny bushes. "Don't move," I called back. "But keep moving."

"That's a paradox," she called after me.

After that there was silence broken only by the crackle of branches as I shoved my way through the bush in Keats' wake. Percy flattened himself against me and finally jumped down to make his way alone. It seemed like ages before we finally came out by a fair-sized pond. It had the barest film of ice overtop, which meant there was an underground creek. Seemed like there were secret creeks running all over this area. You had to be a lifer to know the geography.

"Prints!" I said. "Keats, you're a genius."

Normally he'd take that compliment and mumble with it, but his ruff, tail and ears said we were still in trouble.

I knelt beside the first set of prints and took a photo. They were about the right size for a plump pig, but with the snow it was hard to tell if the tracks had been made by cloven hooves.

"Is it Wilma?" I asked.

Now he offered a mumble in the affirmative. He had a different tone for nearly every animal on the farm and Wilma always got a note of wary respect. Not because he really respected her, but because he knew she wouldn't hesitate to end him if he got in her way.

"Which way, then? It looks like she was going in circles."

Keats picked his way around a bit and then the paw came up again. This time he looked down and I saw crumbs in the snow. Someone must have sprinkled what appeared to be baked goods around here. Looking closely, I saw lots of fine lines in the fluffy snow that could have been made by a broom as someone covered their tracks. They'd left a trail of snacks for a hungry pig—so many that she didn't bother taking it all, which she normally did at home.

"This stinks of a setup," I said, pulling out my phone. "We're going to need help. Pronto."

He whined in eager agreement.

After texting Jilly, I pressed Vivian's number. It went straight to voicemail. As we followed our own tracks back, I tried again and again.

"Maybe her phone's dead," I said. "I warned her not to waste battery."

Keats didn't respond because he was on high alert again and it took all his focus.

"What now?" I asked.

This time he actually growled and *my* hackles came up. Wilma had been loose before—and even rolled me—and he hadn't been this worried.

"I don't like this one bit," I said, picking up the pace. "The sooner we get out of here, the better. I miss Edna. She'd be packing all kinds of heat."

Finally we burst out into the clearing where we'd left Vivian.

"Darn it, she really did keep moving," I said.

Keats charged ahead, unfettered by the thick bush now, and then gave a sharp bark—an announcement.

"What is it?" I asked.

Across the wide clearing, I saw people emerging. Becky was in the lead. She was pointing this way with one hand, telling the camera crew to get a range of shots. In the other was a leash, at the end of which was Byron.

"Where's Vivian?" she called. "I was talking to her and she just cut out suddenly."

"Maybe her phone died," I said. "She was filming me."

I walked ahead of them in the direction Keats had taken and soon found him in another point. This time he was facing a different small pond that had even less ice than the previous one. Near the edge closest to me, some chunks of hard snow had broken off from the shore and floated like mini icebergs in the dark water.

And over one of those mini icebergs hung a ruffled purple scarf.

CHAPTER NINE

"What did you do?" Becky's shriek was so loud I covered my ears with my gloves over my hat. Keats shrank away from the sound and leaned into my legs. Percy turned to Becky, puffed like an adder, and hissed.

"Me? I didn't do anything," I said. "I left her standing safely with you on the phone and followed a lead about my pig. When I got back, she was gone. You're seeing all I know."

"You left Vivian all alone in the woods? What kind of monster are you?"

I lowered my gloves. "Becky, calm down. I wasn't gone long and we don't know what happened. Maybe she's still walking in the bush. One thing that won't help is hysterics. Now, are you or the crew going into the pond, or should I?"

Becky got on the phone with someone and neither man moved.

I looked down at Keats, pleading with him to let me know that the wind had just snatched Vivian's scarf and she'd moved on. He stared up at me with that clear blue eye and I knew the answer.

Unzipping my parka, I dropped it on the snow and then emptied my pockets. Without another word I stepped into the pond. There was no need to tell Keats to stay. He hated water with a burning passion that surpassed even Percy's. I was on my own here.

For a second, I thought the cold would stop my heart, but it didn't. I moved forward feeling the silt sucking at my boots. Plodding toward the floating scarf, I mentally prepared myself to be swept under. That would likely be the end of me, because the crew would probably do nothing but film my demise.

The water reached my waist. My ribcage. My armpits. But that's where it stopped. I was able to grab the scarf easily, if you didn't count how my body was sounding red alerts. I wrapped it around my neck and then waded around, trying to find Vivian's body.

Keats started wailing on the shore. It was a loud keening sound in a pitch I'd never heard before.

"I'm fine, buddy," I said. Only no words came out of my chattering lips, and he continued pleading with me to come to shore. I did as he asked. If Vivian were here, she would be past saving now.

The walk back to shore was both easier and more difficult. I couldn't feel my limbs anymore, and they'd stopped responding to direct orders.

Staggering out, I reached for my phone and yelled, "Did you call the police?"

Becky was still on her phone but Ray and Eric shook their heads. I realized she was talking to the network instead.

I sat down hard in the snow and jabbed at a number on my phone with a finger I couldn't feel.

"Kellan. Can you come out to Gertie's please? Fast."

"What's wrong?" he asked.

"I've run into some trouble. Out near where we found the—you know."

"The caches?" he asked. "Or the Christmas tree?"

"Not the Christmas tree. We're further out than that."

"Looking for Wilma?" he asked. "I doubt she got so far so fast."

"She did, though," I said. "At least, I'm pretty sure the prints are hers. It's possible a wild boar's been around but Keats says it's Wilma."

"*Keats says...?*"

The question came from Becky, not Kellan. He was so used to my quoting Keats that he didn't question anymore. The producer was leaning over me now.

"Who's that?" he asked. "It doesn't sound like Jilly."

"It's Becky Bower. The production assistant on the Faraway Farm show. I had a report that Wilma had been sighted on Gertie's property and they volunteered to help. There were five of us, but now only four. Vivian Crane is gone."

"Gone? Gone where? And why do you sound funny? You're slurring. Have you been drinking?"

"I wish. But no."

I could tell Kellan was on the move now. There were noises in the background and the phone shifted as he put on his coat. "What's really going on, Ivy?"

"I left Vivian standing in a clearing talking to Becky on the phone while I followed Keats into heavy brush. He was signaling a threat and I wanted her to stay safe. I found signs that Wilma had been around, but I came back to get help. By then, Vivian had vanished."

Becky shrieked again. The first screams I'd taken at face value but now they sounded contrived—and deafening at short range. Keats must have thought so, too, because he turned to give her a withering look with his blue eye. Meanwhile Percy scraped at the snow with his front paw. It was his litter box maneuver that usually meant something deadly had happened to someone. In this case, maybe he just wanted to muffle Becky.

"Ivy?" Kellan was running now and I pictured him taking the front stairs at the station two at a time. "What aren't you telling me? I can tell there's more."

"There's a pond," I said. "With open water. Edna says swamps don't freeze fully when there's a creek running underneath. It's possible Vivian tried to walk on the ice and broke through. Her scarf was floating on a little iceberg. So I went in to find her."

"You went into the frozen pond? You'll have hypothermia."

"I'm okay. But I couldn't find her, Kellan. You'll have to—"

"We'll bring the right equipment," he said. "Now get someone to help you back to Gertie's right now and take a lukewarm bath. The others stay put. Understood? We'll talk in a bit."

I managed to press "off" and looked up at Becky. "The chief of police wants one of you to walk me back to Gertie's while the other two stay to show them where to search."

Ray started to come forward but Becky held him back. "We are not leaving Vivian. You got her into this situation, Ivy, and you can take care of yourself."

I wasn't sure I could. It was nearly a half-hour walk to Gertie's. If I collapsed on the way it would just make more trouble for Kellan. Not to mention stressing Keats to the breaking point.

"Becky, we need to help her," Ray said, taking another step forward.

"Do it and you're fired," she said. "Keep rolling. We need evidence for the network."

Pulling on my coat, I clambered to my feet. If I moved around I'd be okay. The police wouldn't be long and someone could take me back.

Staggering around the clearing, with Keats moaning softly at my side, I said, "Just look around while you can, okay? Before people stomp away any signs."

"She's delusional," Becky said. "All the rumors were true."

"Got that right," I said. I did feel drunk and very... floppy. My legs worked but on their own schedule. Finally, I fell over.

"I've got to do something," Ray said. "This isn't right."

"What's not right is what she did to Vivian. And what she might do to us if we don't stick together."

Pushing myself upright again, I flapped a hand. "All good. No worries."

That's when I saw the telltale signs of a scuffle. A bush had been flattened. There were hoof prints all around. A purple leather glove lay on the snow with its middle finger missing. Chewed off, by the looks of things.

"Oh no," I said. "She didn't."

"Didn't *what?*" Becky called.

I wasn't pond-drunk enough to be stupid on camera.

"I think Vivian fell and rolled in right about here," I said. "Maybe she fainted. She hadn't eaten today."

"Vivian always fasts till dinner."

Becky started to walk toward me and I raised my hand to stop her from contaminating the crime scene I was already jeopardizing. If I fell again, I'd try to do it in the other direction.

"Stop," I said. "Where's Byron?"

"Byron? Who cares about the dog? The network is going to have a fit about all this."

My teeth were chattering uncontrollably now but I could still hear the roar of an engine.

"The cops are coming," I said.

It wasn't the cops though. Not yet. The ATV carried one octogenarian in a poncho and another in fatigues. The sight of them gave me the permission I needed to faint.

CHAPTER TEN

I spent the rest of the day reluctantly recovering from my frosty dip while Cori and an expanding group of volunteers continued the search for Wilma and now Byron, as well. I didn't hold out much hope for success as the police had chased the rescuers off Gertie's property and Becky had blocked them from the old Swenson place. It seemed likely that both animals were located on one of the two properties. I was more worried about Byron than Wilma. She'd been on the run before and was tough and cagey. Byron seemed like a sweetheart and he was new to the area. He probably couldn't find his way home to his small flock.

Jilly came in from the kitchen with hot chocolate she'd made from scratch. I'd turned down soup and even coffee, but I couldn't pass this up. Mom complained it was too rich for her tastes, but to date nothing Jilly prepared had ever been too rich or too sweet for me. These days, with all the farm work, I needed all the calories I could get.

"Does Kellan really believe Wilma pushed Vivian into the pond?" she asked, lifting my slippered feet, sitting at the end of the couch and setting them in her lap. "It seems extreme. Even for Wilma."

"If she did I'm sure it wasn't intentional," I said. "I mean, Wilma is always willing to knock someone down—especially me. But I don't think she'd deliberately drown someone." My fingers reached for Keats again and found only air. Kellan had enlisted not only the dog but also the cat to aid in the search. It had caused a little tension between him and Cori. They'd both wanted Keats on their team. The thought made me smile. As a slight and bookish kid, I'd been the last to be chosen for any team outside of math club at school. It was nice that my dog and even my cat were the cool kids. But I didn't like giving them up, even temporarily. I trusted Kellan but these weren't just pets... they were pieces of me. I wouldn't be whole until they were home.

Jilly took my twitching fingers and squeezed. "You still have me. And if you like, I could go down and get Clippers. I don't want a horse inside, but he is housetrained and the best of the options."

I squeezed her hand back and grinned. It was a big concession. Too big. So I shook my head. "I'm fine, really. The shock is just physical. Edna got me out of there before I had to see... well, anything."

Gertie and her rifle had stayed. Indeed, only Gertie and her rifle had managed to keep the crew from filming as the police trawled the pond and ultimately recovered Vivian. By then, the body was covered in silt, Kellan said, and long past resuscitation.

Asher escorted the crew off the property and Gertie escorted Asher. The only cop she trusted, apparently, was Kellan.

"What do *you* think happened?" Jilly asked.

I sighed and squeezed her hand even harder. "I think Kellan's going to find signs of foul play."

"What makes you think that?"

"The usual. Keats was in a state and he wouldn't get so fussed about Wilma. I've seen him when that pig is riled dozens of times and while he's wary, he never hit red alert. All his flags were flying today. And Percy... well, he did the litter box thing. He made quite a job of it after she was recovered. Kellan made a point of letting me know."

"Maybe Percy does that with all dead things."

"Maybe. But I've only noticed it around murder victims, ceramic or real." I shrugged. "Anything the animals do is open to interpretation, of course. I'm still learning their languages."

She slumped back against the cushy leather and slid down. "Not again. Oh, Ivy... not again."

"Let's not get too worked up about it till we know for sure," I said. "When Kellan drops off the pets we'll get a better idea."

"At least it wasn't here on the farm," Jilly said. "Not that I wished Vivian ill anywhere." She blew a few curly tendrils out of her eyes. "I wish they'd never come here with their silly show."

"I expect they'll pack up and go as soon as the police close the case. And good riddance."

"Ivy!" Mom's voice blasted from the second floor. "There's a car coming up the driveway. It's a Mercedes."

"Did she move to a front room?" I asked Jilly. "One of the suites?"

Jilly nodded sheepishly. "It happened when we were out searching for Wilma. Someone brought over her sewing machine and clothes, and she needed more space."

"Why didn't you tell me? The more settled she gets the harder it will be to yank her out by the roots."

"I know. I just didn't want you to be more upset since we couldn't find the pig."

"Which sibling betrayed me?" I said. "Someone's going to pay."

She shrugged and I believed she didn't know. The main attractions here were probably Jilly's food and Jilly herself. My best friend was the sweet, respectful daughter Mom hadn't fostered among her own five girls.

"You rest while I deal with this," Jilly said. "If it's Becky, I may very well chase her off the porch with a broom."

"I've got a better idea," I said, picking up my phone and sending a quick text. "She's very persistent and very accusatory, when all I did was ask Vivian to stay put for a few minutes and stay safe."

As fast as Jilly moved, Mom managed to beat her to the door. "What do you want, Becky Bower?" she demanded. "You have some nerve coming over here after what you did to my daughter. She could have died trying to rescue your boss. Meanwhile all you did was stand there filming."

"Mom!" I was willing to let Jilly fight my battles, but Mom would only layer more battles on top of them. Wrapping the wool throw around my shoulders, I walked into the front hall. "Becky, I'm not up to chatting right now. And I know Chief Harper told you to stay at... at your set. He'll be here before long and you'll want to get back before that happens."

Becky tried to come in uninvited but Mom blocked her with ease. She was small but still mighty. Raising six kids alone had made her both alert and agile. "Out. You heard Ivy."

"Ouch. Hey." Becky hopped around. "You stepped on my foot."

"An accident," Mom said. "But your foot *was* on my daughter's property."

I pressed my lips together to hold back a smile. Mom was wearing stilettos, as she typically did even at home. She never wanted to be caught with her heels down.

"It's not funny," Becky said, glaring at me. "Do you think I want to be here?"

"Probably not," I said. "So don't let us keep you."

"I was sent by the network. The executive producers of the show have met to talk about what happened."

"I'm sure it was a terrible shock to lose Vivian," I said. "My sympathies to all of you."

"I refuse to accept your so-called sympathies when you let this happen." She tried to force her way past Mom again and got her other foot stomped in the process. "Stop that!"

"Then stop insinuating my daughter had anything to do with Vivian Crane's demise. It was a regrettable accident, to be sure, but no one knows what happened. And everyone warned you that country life can be dangerous."

"I'm sorry about the show ending," I said. "Well, not really. But I am sorry about Vivian. Truly."

"That's why I'm here," she said, feinting right and then making a last push to get past Mom. This time she succeeded only because Mom couldn't risk damaging her manicure by clutching the door. She always said sewing and barbering were so hard on her nails that she couldn't engage in other risky activities. Like housework. Or cooking. Here, all of that would be done for her.

Becky thought her fight was over, but Jilly was no pushover. "Whatever it is, spit it out so that Ivy can rest. You let her go into that pond and just stood there. She could have died."

"Well, she didn't obviously. And that's why the network wants Ivy to take over the show in the starring role."

"What?" Jilly, Mom and I spoke at once.

"The show must go on, of course. Ratings for the first episode were excellent and you're the logical choice to step into Vivian's shoes. You know farming and livestock. Jilly can cover cooking and entertaining. And this one"—she elbowed Mom—"can cover sewing. I'm sure the rest of your family has plenty of expertise to share."

There was a light in Mom's eyes but I beat her to the punch.

"Becky, that's appalling. Shameless. I wouldn't participate before and I certainly won't now. It would be disrespectful to Vivian's memory."

"They said you could name your price. We all know how you've struggled to find your footing here, and no wonder. But all that could change now. You'll be rich."

I stared at her. "That doesn't tempt me for a second. I spent ten years compromising my principles in the corporate world. I don't need to do it anymore. Not when I'm rich already in every way that counts."

"We all compromise our principles. Even you," she said.

I thought about arguing but she wasn't wrong. "I have and probably will again for the sake of my animals. But I won't profit off a woman's passing."

"I don't like the idea any more than you do. But the execs saw the footage of you going into the water. They saw your connection with the dog and cat. And they said they've got to have you." She shrugged. "They usually get their way."

"I'll see you out," I said, coming forward. I was taller than either of the others but the wool throw diminished my presence. "Please go back to your place and stay there. It's really best to listen to the police in these situations."

"Like you ever do," she said, stepping out on the porch.

Over her shoulder, I saw Ray and Eric going from pasture to pasture, filming.

"Hey," I yelled. "Get off my property with those cameras."

"Or what?" Becky said. "You'll call the police? They've got their hands full right now."

"I don't need the police," I said. "I have something just as good."

The roar of an ATV reached us and Becky finally quailed. "Oh no, it's that zombie hunter wack-job."

"Take 'em out, Edna," I called, sweeping my arm toward their car. Vivian's car. It was indecent that they were driving it only hours after she stopped needing it.

Edna shouted "yeehaw" and circled the two men. It was good to see them run, cradling their cameras.

"Careful," Becky called, running down the stairs. "Those cost a bomb. The execs will have your head." She turned back with a sheepish glance. "I didn't mean it like that."

"Less talk more run," Edna bellowed, driving onto the front walk to round up Becky and press her toward the Mercedes. "Are your shots up to date, Becks? Because you never know what you might catch on a farm."

"I have insurance," the producer yelled, starting to run.

"Ah, sweet country life," I said to Jilly and Mom, as I clutched the blanket. "Not always peaceful, but never dull."

CHAPTER ELEVEN

The great thing about manure was that it was a constantly renewable resource. When winter set in, I worried that my pile behind the barn would freeze, and I'd have to find a new hobby to relieve stress. Wood-splitting was a good contender, but my nearest and dearest expressed concerns about my dexterity with an ax. It seemed better to wait till my brain injury had healed fully before getting too ambitious with sharp tools.

It turned out to be a non-issue anyway. The manure never did freeze. Every day, there were steaming new piles to layer on top and with the various chemical reactions, things kept percolating. I could pick up my shovel anytime and turn my worries into compost. When the pile got too high, Charlie used the tractor to dismantle it and haul it away to neighboring crop-farmers. They claimed I had some of the finest dung in hill country and I took a fair bit of pride in that. Compliments were few and far between in my new life. Or even my old life, where high prize was being called a shark or killer.

Slamming the spade into the pile with my boot, I turned the manure. It felt good to do something constructive after a very crappy day. Next summer, my efforts here would produce tomatoes, corn and cheery pumpkins on roadside stands.

A flurry of black, white and orange caught my eye as my beloveds arrived home. Keats delivered a series of sharp barks to get me to come down. He preferred getting his white paws dirty on his own terms. Percy wouldn't come anywhere near me during or long after manure management. It was the price I paid for sanity.

"Coming, coming," I said, walking down what Jilly called my "stairway to heaven."

Keats was in a frenzy. With all the twists, turns, moans and grumbles, I had to kneel to shower him with attention and praise. He was "talking" so fast, I couldn't keep up. I tried hugging him, because *I* needed the hug, but he was a whirling dervish.

I looked up at Kellan. "What is he saying?"

"You're asking me? I barely speak dog."

"Well, he's got quite a story to tell and I bet you could tell it faster."

Kellan smiled. "He signed our canine confidentiality agreement. Working with a police force comes at a price. I hope it doesn't come between you two."

"Never." Keats calmed down enough to not only permit the hug but wrap his paws around my neck. I stood up, holding him like a toddler. It was awkward but I buried my face in his neck and mumbled, "Missed you too, buddy. Manure was all I had left."

Sighing, I put the dog down and he transformed into Chief Sheepdog of Runaway Farm. As he began his evening rounds, a high-pitched whine told me Wilma's pen would remain empty. Cori and the gang hadn't turned up anything new, either.

Kellan leaned against Florence's stall. The old blind mare still took a nip at him now and then and usually he was more cautious. "You shouldn't be working so hard," he said. "Not tonight. That was quite an ordeal."

"It sure was, which is why I needed to be out here. It was either this or find less healthy distractions."

He shook his head. "I don't know how healthy it is to suck in toxic fumes all the time."

"Did you know a horse produces nine tons of manure in a year?" I asked. "Over a lifetime, it's—"

"Never mind. I get your point. No more lectures."

"You've had quite an ordeal today, too," I said. "Worse than mine."

"Yeah, but ordeals are my job. I have a high threshold for them, whereas you're still in training."

"It has been a bit much. I'd like to speak to whoever's in charge of ordeals in this town."

He laughed and we both seemed to relax in the same moment. "Can I give you a hug?" he asked.

"Can you handle the risk of passing out?"

"Yeah. Yeah, I can. Just let me ease in slowly. It's like sinking into a steaming geyser."

"A geyser? Now that is flattering."

"A hot spring then. Sulphurous, yet therapeutic."

I slipped into his arms and he squeezed me good and tight. "You say the sweetest things."

"I know. I got training on that in Ordeal School. People who handle ordeals for a living don't always show their best side at home."

Pressing my face into his chest, I mumbled, "I like all your sides. Even the lecturing side. I know you worry about me."

He kissed my hair a little gingerly but the sentiment made up for it. "There's a lot to worry about. You always seem to end up in the wrong place at the wrong time."

"The animals lead me to the strangest places. Today I went from that terrible scene at the pond to being courted by a TV network. You could be hugging the brand new star of Faraway Farm."

All the effervescence left the air leaving only... fumes. I had taken the joke too far.

Kellan took a step back and leaned against the stall again. "You're not. *They're* not. This is an open investigation."

"I'm not, don't worry. And what kind of investigation? Criminal?"

"I'd prefer not to comment," he said. "But I suppose Keats will tell you anyway. Or worse, he'll lead you places I don't want you to go."

"So... Vivian didn't just fall into that pond."

"It appears not. She was definitely pushed."

I covered my face with my hands for a second and then split my fingers to peek at him. "Please tell me it wasn't Wilma."

"That has yet to be determined. Wilma—or a pig just like her—was at the scene. You saw the glove. It's likely she'll poop purple tomorrow because Vivian's other glove was missing, too."

"Were her injuries consistent with a pig attack?"

"I'm not sure exactly what injuries *are* consistent with a pig attack," he said. "But I'm leaning toward a human assailant. Vivian had a contusion on the back of her head. Probably never saw it coming. My best guess at this point is that she was trying to catch the pig when someone caught her."

"Oh no! I hate to think of her grappling with Wilma alone and leaving herself vulnerable to another attack."

"You know how these things go, unfortunately. The pig opened the door and someone was waiting to walk through it."

"But who would want Vivian Crane dead?" I asked. "I mean, she was a bully, and probably stepped on a few people on her way up. But who would take it that far?"

"Too soon to say. No sign of her phone. We spent the day examining every stick and snowflake in the area but there wasn't much to go on. There appeared to be some boot prints but they'd been obscured and ended in a stream. Keats did his best, I'll give him that."

"He showed you the pig food?" I asked.

"Yeah. Clearly, Wilma isn't going to starve. Her tracks ended in a stream, too. By that time, she was leaving chunks of food behind. The pig was actually full up."

"I've never seen her turn down food. *Never.* She was starved in her youth and vowed never to be hungry again. Who would be feeding her, and why?"

"We'll find out. In the meantime, Keats practically cried when she took to the water and we lost her scent."

"That's his Achilles heel," I said. "He just can't do water."

"No complaints about his contributions. He was a big help and I appreciated his freelancing with me today." Florence made her move and snatched his fuzzy-flapped police-issue hat. His half-hearted attempt to reclaim it proved how tired he was. "And I appreciate that you trusted me with your pets when you probably needed them yourself."

"I had Jilly, thank goodness. How did Percy do?"

"Spent most of the day on my shoulder, much to the merriment of my team."

"I'm sorry. Percy prefers to conserve his energy, especially in snow. He lets Keats do the heavy lifting and then sails in to show him up when needed. I should have brought him home."

"Nah. Lightening the mood wasn't a bad thing," he said, smiling. "We've had a heavy few months in the department of ordeals."

"So true. I hoped the new year would end that." I opened the door to the horse stall and recovered Kellan's hat. Or at least most of it. "I'll give this a wash and Mom can stitch it back up for you. She's brought her machine over and set up a studio in the best suite."

His smile vanished. "Is Dahlia living here now?"

"The inn is under subtle siege. She's moving things in bit by bit till I call her on it. And I will, when there are guests in need of that suite. For the moment, I don't mind that much because Jilly has a calming influence on her and Daisy and Poppy are here a lot, too. Many hands make light work with Mom."

He laughed in apparent relief and slung his arm around me. "I'd better go. There are many miles of paperwork to walk before I sleep. Seeing you for a few minutes will make that more bearable."

"Seeing you makes everything more bearable," I said, walking him out to the police SUV.

Offering affection so freely still made me feel dreadfully exposed but it was getting easier. Hiding my emotions was a skill I'd honed since childhood and made me the grim reaper of HR I became. But I could and would change. Ordeal School was making short work of what I thought to be immutable. Well, that and my animals. Full ark, full heart.

He opened the door and started the SUV. Then he got back out to give me a kiss that chased the last of the icy pond's chill from my toes.

I stood grinning in the headlights as he slid behind the wheel again. That grin turned to laughter as something bright and fluffy landed on his shoulders and he gave a little man-shriek.

"You *can* get good help," I said, taking the cat he handed over. "But sometimes they don't know when to stop."

"Sleep well," he said, closing the door. "Dream about staying out of trouble."

I laughed again. "That is a nice dream."

CHAPTER TWELVE

Kellan's headlights merged with another car's as it drove up the lane. I thought it might be Asher coming to check on Jilly because it was late to be anyone other than family.

A sedan pulled up to the spot Kellan had just left and the window rolled down.

"Mayor Martingale! What a surprise."

"A welcome one, I hope." Poking her meticulously highlighted head out the window, she greeted Percy and then Keats when he trotted over from the barn. The white tuft of his tail waved a warm welcome.

"Keats speaks for me," I said. "We missed you after Christmas."

The mayor and her husband, as well as her brother and his family, had stayed for several days over the holiday and we'd had a wonderful time.

"You can expect a reunion every year," she said. "My niece can't stop talking about you."

"How's it going with the puppy?" I asked.

"I've never seen that kid happier. You did a good thing in making that happen, Ivy."

I smiled. Of all the good things I'd done or tried to do since my homecoming, connecting that teen with a dog was the easiest and most joyful. "She's a great kid. I can't wait to see her again."

"She's angling to come back sooner now that Faraway Farm is shooting here."

"*Was* shooting here. It was short-lived." I closed my eyes. "Poor choice of words. I'm exhausted."

"Not surprising. I was impressed by what you did today."

"You already heard?"

"Heard and saw."

"Saw? How?"

She pulled her phone out of her purse and then cued something up. Holding the phone out, she let me watch myself walk into a pond while my dog threw back his head and howled. The sound was off but Keats still cocked his head and stared with his eerie blue eye.

"The network emailed the footage during our call today," she said. "Obviously they're very concerned about what happened to Vivian Crane."

"We all are," I said. "That's why Chief Harper was just here."

She lowered the phone and grinned. "I saw he was resuscitating you. It seemed like overkill, since the video showed you making your way out of the pond under your own steam."

"Very funny." A flush lit up my body in a not unwelcome wave of heat. "It's not against the law for the chief to kiss his girlfriend after a long hard day. Especially when she's had a long hard day, too."

"Relax, Ivy, I'm just teasing. Obviously you scored some major points by trying to find Vivian when her crew refused. The network is going to contact you directly to apologize."

"No need," I said. "Most people would have done the same."

The mayor laughed. "It sounds like you actually believe that."

"It's what I want to believe. Most people in my circle would have tried. It's such a shame I was too late." I scuffed at the snow with one boot. "Such a shame I left her alone for a few minutes while I looked for Wilma. My pig. It sounds like they may have had an altercation."

"I heard about the gloves," Mayor Martingale said. "But Chief Harper is confident the autopsy will show Wilma isn't to blame."

"I sure hope so," I said. "I mean... I'm sorry about what happened, but I don't want my pig to be responsible."

"Either way, Wilma's going to be on the hook until the matter is resolved," the mayor said.

"Why? You said it's not her fault."

She dropped the phone into her purse and ran her hand through her hair. It fell right back into place because she had the perfect cut, especially for a politician. Somehow, it was easier to trust someone with perfect hair. It suggested they weren't tossed around by the winds or the ponds the rest of us faced. She had things locked down.

"I'll be honest because you deserve that from me," she said. "I need a scapegoat, Ivy. Or in this case, a scape-pig. Two men were murdered in Clover Grove just six weeks ago, and others before that. The townspeople are understandably rattled. As their leader, I need to keep them calm, and if they believe there's another murderer at large, it's an uphill battle."

"A rogue pig is easier?"

"Of course. We're country folk. Rogue animals are common enough. You can defend yourself against a crazed animal better than a crazed human."

My breath came out in short gusts that gave away my nerves. "If someone shoots my pig, Mayor, I don't know what I'll do."

"No one will shoot your pig. I will convey the message loud and clear that she is to be found and delivered safely into your hands. There will be a very good reward."

I switched to yoga breathing—in for four, out for four. Keats had positioned himself with his ears in easy reach and I availed myself of them now. "Mayor, that's all well and good, but I'll become the scapegoat. The scape-farmer. People will talk about how my loose pig—the one I couldn't control—killed a TV star."

Now she blew out a steamy sigh. "I know, and I'm sorry, but you know well that they already talk. It's just one more story to add to your already thick file."

"That's not fair!"

"It most certainly isn't," she said. "Not when you've done so much to resolve crime in this area. You've put your own life on the line time and again—so often that I've put your name forward for a good citizenship award. That will help with public perceptions, I'm sure."

"No one cares about things like that. They'd rather believe negative press."

"Give me a little credit for understanding how human nature works, Ivy. And understanding this town. I've lived here a long time."

"I know. With all due respect, stories like this will affect my livelihood. People won't come to the inn if they think they'll be next to die under Wilma."

"They will, though. How many guests have I sent you in recent weeks?"

"A dozen or so. And thank you."

"I've recommended Runaway Inn to several upcoming meetings and conventions. A year from now you'll be turning guests away."

"That seems too good to be true from where I stand now," I said. "And a year's a long time to live on hope."

"Well, there is a faster way…" Her eyes sharpened in the reflection from the dashboard. "If you're open to it."

Keats mumbled a warning and I felt the reverberation through my fingertips.

"I'm open to any of your ideas," I said. "As long as they don't involve that TV show."

"Ivy, I'm sure you can see how much it would help your inn—

your animals—if you said yes to the network. It wouldn't take much work on your end." She gestured behind her. "They can move the sign to your lane. Faraway Farm. It has a lovely alliteration and that's exactly what you should do: get as far away from your reputation as you can. This show will completely rebuild you in the public's perception."

My laugh came out as a harsh bray somewhat reminiscent of Bocelli the donkey. "Again, with all due respect, it feels like this has more to do with politics than my farm. The show could bring business to Clover Grove, I'm sure. It would put us on the map and help us compete with Dorset Hills for tourist dollars."

She shrugged. "It's all politics. You know that. I'm sure it was also true in your corporate life."

"Which I left, after having the soul sucked out of me."

"Your soul is very much intact and the animals here are the proof of it. Look at that dog. He'd do anything for you." Her white teeth flashed and I realized she'd gotten veneers since being elected. "Even star in a TV show. Keats is already a celebrity and the network is willing to pay him a regular actor's wages. Think about what the money could do to maintain this ark of yours."

"It's not about money."

"It's always about money," she said. "One way or the other. Money and politics. Politics and money. The key is finding a balance between them you can live with."

"That's not in my personal equation. Rescuing Keats forced me to take stock of my life and I ended up here, working with animals. Shoveling manure. Saving the odd life if I can. My philosophy, what I truly believe at my core, is that my service and integrity will carry me through without having to compromise my integrity."

She gave me a pitying look. "That's naïve, Ivy."

"No one's called me naïve in a long time, Mayor."

I snapped my fingers at Percy, who was crouching to make a leap at the mayor's window. Tempting as it was, I didn't want him to deliver one of his special 10-claw scalp massages as he landed. The mayor was doing what she thought was best for the town, no matter the cost to me. That's what got her elected. But I didn't need to go along for that ride. There were other ways to make Clover Grove great that didn't involve reality TV.

"Let's talk more tomorrow," she said.

"Thanks for coming by. I'll be back hunting for Wilma tomorrow."

"Just think about what I said. And in the meantime, if there's anything you and your Dream Team can do to resolve the situation with Vivian, you'd have town council's gratitude."

"The chief of police has that well in hand, I'm sure," I said.

"I wish I could trust him as you do. I have more faith in Keats, I'm afraid."

"Don't say that. Kellan is wonderful at his job."

"Spoken like a woman defending her boyfriend. If you believed that, you wouldn't interfere with his cases."

Keats moved into position under my hand again and infused me with enough calming energy to see she was manipulating me. Normally I wouldn't need my dog to show me that, but the relationship complexities were still fairly new territory.

"Mayor Martingale, it sounds like you don't know me at all. I interfere because I *want* to. Keats and Percy and I have an insatiable curiosity and energy to burn." I smiled down at the dog. "All that said, I have complete faith in Chief Harper. He just gets answers in different ways—ways that don't jeopardize the public as mine might. At least, that's what he tells me."

She put the car in gear and started rolling backward. "Try putting that curiosity to work for Vivian. For the town. You have my full support."

If I had her full support, she wouldn't be scapegoating my pig or me. But I wasn't surprised. My naïveté about how the world worked vanished long ago. Sometimes it seemed like I was born jaded and the only things reversing that were Keats and the farm. Salvation could be found in manure and the producers of it.

"Bye now," I called. "I'm going back to my dung heap."

"Oh, Ivy," she called back. "You'll need to watch what you say if you hope to last on that show."

"Careful," I called. "There's a—"

She was reversing too fast and erratically and hit the big pothole hard.

I'd have to think about filling that again. But there was no hurry.

CHAPTER THIRTEEN

"Well, boys," I said, as we drove toward town the next morning, "this is the first time we've had a direct order to sleuth. That practically makes us private detectives, doesn't it?"

Keats mumbled a definitive yes to that while Percy just curled up in a tighter ball on the passenger seat. He had less drive than Keats and me and some of it had already fizzled after our morning rounds. I had no doubt, however, that the cat would bring his A game when needed.

We only had a couple of hours to spare before meeting Cori and the search party. Kellan had declared Gertie's property and the neighboring ones off limits until he was satisfied with *his* investigation. It didn't make sense to go much farther afield when we knew the pig had been in the area the day before and there was food to keep her there.

Now we needed to find Byron, too. I couldn't help wondering if he'd joined ranks with the pig while we were dealing with the Vivian situation. A guardian dog normally wouldn't stray from his official charges, but perhaps he'd found another animal that needed his protection. A framed and defamed pig.

"Kellan won't be happy with our new designation as the Mayor's

Task Force," I said. "Hopefully he'll get the case solved before we need to do very much. Her biggest priority may be solving Vivian's murder but mine is finding the animals." I released my death grip on the gear shift to rest my hand on Keats. I avoided touching his jacket, which just made him cringe. "We'd better be the Mayor's *Secret* Task Force. Hearing that the mayor puts more faith in us than the police might hurt Kellan's pride. We can't do that."

Keats panted a no-no-no. He respected Kellan more every day, especially now that he was practically on the police payroll. In fact, Kellan couldn't have picked a better way to win the dog over. Assisting the chief was a great honor and privilege, especially for a sheepdog. Normally only German or Belgian shepherds got the nod for that.

"The mayor's just manipulating us anyway," I said. "She's probably trying to foster dissent between Kellan and me to get what she wants. I don't even blame her for it. She's not pretending to be anything other than what she is, namely a politician."

The dog's ears flattened and he gave me a steely stare. *He* blamed her for it. No doubt he thought the only things coming between Kellan and me should be him and Percy.

"Don't worry," I said. "She won't win this game. I'll poke around to see what I can find out about Vivian to serve my own goals. I want that production to leave town, and the sooner the better. Until then, she'll keep trying to sell me on that show. But she can't make me do it."

His expression looked doubtful now and he mumbled a warning.

"Oh, I hear you, buddy. The mayor has ways. The network has ways. For all I know they could be holding Wilma hostage until I comply. And they could do much worse." I blew out a big sigh and then did a couple of rounds of four-count yoga breathing. Panic was the enemy of the Secret Task Force. "Here's my take on it," I continued. "They could twist my arm hard enough by threatening my animals. It's my weak point. What they don't realize is that hiring me would tank their ratings. Thanks to that concussion, I'm a wild card and a liability. All I'd have to do is be myself and the show would fire me and cast another new farmer. Total authenticity is my ace in the hole."

Keats' pant turned to a hearty ha-ha-ha that was loud enough to rouse Percy, who stretched in his little yellow jacket and flexed his claws against my leg. I could feel them through my fleece-lined overalls.

"Percy, must you? I'm always covered in little pinpricks. It's not nice to puncture your meal ticket."

We pulled into the parking lot outside Mandy's Country Store.

"Just between us, boys, my money's on Becky. I bet she hired someone to take Vivian out. After suffering years of bullying, Becky probably turned. Or one of the camera guys. Or all three."

Percy stepped into his carrier so that he could come inside. I never let him wander free in places that served food. I was already pushing my luck with Keats, but he normally sat with me rather than flaunting his fluff like freewheeling Percy.

The investigation began, as others had, with pie. We took our usual place in the corner seat along the long laminate bar at the front window. There was a shelf underneath where Percy's carrier allowed him a view of both parking lot and store. Keats sat beside the stool, muzzle swiveling.

I'd timed my arrival perfectly. Within the hour, regulars would come in to nurse a coffee for hours, do the crossword puzzle and gossip. If I wanted privacy and Mandy's undivided attention, it was best to get there right after she opened. It was early for pie, and I'd already had breakfast, but that didn't stop me. Mandy raised her eyebrows as I came in and nodded to confirm my standing order. Moments later, she slid a double wedge of her classic coconut cream pie in front of me. It had dairy. It had protein. It had calcium. Practically health food.

She hopped onto the high stool beside mine and said, "If you're here this early for pie, you must be up to no good."

I laughed. It was nice that we could joke comfortably with each other again. After what had happened with Lloyd Boyce, the dogcatcher, I'd sworn never to come in here, let alone be friends. She'd hidden facts from me with catastrophic results, but she truly regretted it. Now she tried to make up for it by collecting and sharing whatever intel she could glean from her customers. In short order, she'd become our star informer. And on top of everything else, this expert baker had pie on her side. That was *her* ace in the hole because it primed my forgiveness pump. So I'd done what I'd once thought impossible and put the dogcatcher betrayal behind me. Mandy was a good person who'd been in a difficult situation. Nowadays, I tried hard to see the other perspective before judging. Particularly if that person was a genius with coconut cream.

"Maybe I am," I said. "I'm sure you heard what happened yesterday."

She shrugged her slim shoulders. Mandy probably burned as many calories worrying as I did mucking stalls. "Couldn't really avoid it," she said. "It was even on the national news. No need for the grapevine this time."

"But the grapevine adds local flavor. More sensational than anything Hollywood has to offer."

Now she laughed. "Speculation is running rampant. I think people are hoping reporters will descend on us. Local theories are more farfetched than ever."

"I assume a pig attack tops the list?"

"It tops the list of routine possibilities. But there's so much more this time. Ghosts. Witches. Even aliens. Because there were no prints, apparently." She sipped her own coffee. "Is that part true?"

"I didn't see any prints but Wilma's. But then I wasn't at my best after my dip in the pond. Turns out hypothermia dulls my perception."

"I would think so. I'm amazed you bounced back so quickly."

"No choice. I've got a farm to run and a pig to find. Not to mention Byron, the show's dog. He's on the lam, too."

"So, how can I help?" she asked, raising delicate eyebrows. Her once dirty blonde hair was highlighted now and her makeup was on point. Running this place was transforming the shy girl into a confident woman day by day.

I took my first mouthful of pie and closed my eyes to savor it before answering. "The usual. I'm assuming people visited here in the weeks before word of the show got out. What did you notice?"

Nodding, she crossed her legs. "The locations people came first. Weeks ago, just days after what happened at Vinnie Swenson's. They were trying to secure the property for the show but the estate was tied up until one of Vinnie's cousins came forward. Money solved everything, of course."

"The network really splashed out on this. Kind of strange for a so-called simple farm show."

"That kitchen, right?" Mandy said. "The things I could make..." She laughed again. "The things I *did* make so they could pass them off as Vivian's. It was already bringing me good business."

I continued to work through the pie. "I guess the whole town got its hopes up for that."

"Yes and no. Some were excited about possibilities and others worried about how they might be portrayed. With people like Becky Bower, you can't control the spin."

My throat tightened for a moment but another forkful of coconut cream eased the tension. "No, you cannot. So, who was worried? Other than me?"

"The Langman sisters, for starters. They're already on the outs with nearly everyone after finding and hoarding the treasure they illegally dug up at the Swensons'. Most people believed it should have gone into the town coffers for the good of the community, rather than the Langmans' wallet."

"I'm with them there. Gertie's donating a lot of her so-called treasure to the new recreation center, as well as animal rescue. She calls it laundering through good causes. There's no way of knowing how much Heddy and Kaye pilfered and hid."

"Exactly. So their social currency isn't high and they were worried the story would come up on the show."

I set the fork down at the halfway point. It was important to respect the double slice—to take a moment and give thanks for the abundance of the universe. That way there might always be more pie. "Who else is upset?" I asked.

"Beverly Roxton. She's still in a tizzy over what happened at Christmas but can't keep a low profile because the show enlisted Dr. Roxton to be the show's veterinarian. I think he sees it as a chance to clear the family name, but Beverly doesn't trust him not to get into trouble."

"Sounds like people who've taken some kicks in the rumor mill are worried about being profiled on the show."

"They're right to worry. I overheard Becky and the crew talking about the show's evolution. The goal was to start out charming and then gradually expose the town's seedy underbelly. They called Clover Grove 'Crimetown USA.'"

"Lovely. I figured as much. Seedy probably brings better ratings." I picked up my fork again. "I wish the mayor realized that. She might not be so generous with her tax incentives."

Mandy looked out at the empty parking lot and sighed. "I guess it's all a moot point now. With Vivian gone, the show can't go on."

"Don't be so sure of that," I said. "The network is trying to connive a way to continue."

She glanced back at me quickly. "That would be tacky and disrespectful to Vivian's memory. Won't that bring bad press?"

"They've got the budget for spin doctors. My hope is that exposing the murderer might be enough to drive them away for good.

Especially if it's someone on their own team. It seemed like there wasn't much love lost for Vivian."

"I hate to speak ill of the dead but she wasn't a kind woman. I met up with her both here and on set and each time she pretended not to know me or even see me. Becky, on the other hand, liked to browbeat me about my pastry. Not flaky enough. Vivian herself could make a better pie, apparently."

I dropped the fork on the plate with a clatter. "Blasphemy! No one makes a better pie than you, Mandy McCain. I've been to the finest pie baking establishments in this country and beyond. Your pastry is perfection and your coconut cream sublime."

She flushed and grinned at the same time. "No need to lay it on so thick, Ivy. You know you're in the double slice club for life."

Picking up the fork, I relished the last mouthful. "Who else is in that club?"

"Only Kellan and Asher," she said. "And Kellan can't handle the double hit like you can."

"I know. Poor man only eats for one, whereas I need to fuel a farm." I washed the pie down with a few gulps of coffee. "I'm aiming for the triple slice club, just so you know."

"That's half a pie. I'm afraid you'd be sick."

"You underestimate me, Mandy."

"Never." She slipped off her stool and collected a pepperoni stick for Keats and a couple of small treats that were like crack for cats. "There's something else, Ivy. I hope you already know but I need to be sure. It's about your family."

"Oh?" That's what I said aloud. Inside I said, "*Oh no.*"

"I'm sure it's nothing, but I've witnessed a couple of private meetings that may or may not have been dates. Not here, though. At Pages and Pastries, and the Berry Good Café."

"Dates? With whom?"

"One of the camera guys. Ray Faux, I think his name is. He seems nice enough, at least in comparison to the others."

"Ray? Mom is dating a man half her age?" I downed the rest of my coffee. "Why does that even surprise me?"

"Not your mom this time, Ivy."

I stared at her over the cup. "Who else would sell me out by dating that crew?"

Mandy cringed at having to deliver the bad news. "Poppy. In her defense, we've talked about how hard it is to find good guys in this town."

I swallowed hard, realizing there may indeed be an upper limit on my pie capacity. A betrayal by family could make even my strong stomach protest.

"Yesterday Ray Faux was willing to let me drown or freeze to death on Becky's orders. He is not a good guy."

"She didn't know that then," Mandy said. "I'm the first to say people do stupid things for love. Even when it's not really love. Poppy will regret it, just like I did."

A couple of six-count yoga breaths helped me regulate my mouth before I spoke. "Thank you for everything, Mandy. I'd always rather know than be surprised later." Sliding off the stool, I slung Percy's carrier over my shoulder and headed for the door. My fingers were already on the handle when I told Keats to wait. I turned to Mandy and said, "I'd better take a couple of cookies to settle my stomach. It's going to be a long day."

CHAPTER FOURTEEN

M om hopped onto her stool at Daisy's kitchen counter with relative ease. For once she'd worn a skirt with some traction. Normally she was sliding all over with flailing heels and one of us had to brace her. Today, however, she hooked her stilettos over the footrail, steadied herself, and then reached for the mug of coffee Daisy offered.

Inspecting the mug, Mom rolled her eyes. All of Daisy's dishes were white, including the mugs, but the one in Mom's hand was bright red. It would hide waxy lipstick stains.

"World's Best Mom," I said, reading the words on the side. "Well, aren't you special?"

Mom glared at me and then Daisy. "You all make it perfectly clear that I'm anything but every time I sit on this stool."

"Don't take it that way," I said. "We're just trying to keep you on your game. What's family for?"

Iris, Violet and Poppy laughed, but Jilly gave Asher a look to keep him from joining in. She tried to back Mom when it didn't undermine me.

"Buying me a dollar store mug isn't going to make me strive for more," Mom said.

Daisy smiled as she spritzed cleanser onto the pristine counter and gave it a wipe. "Oh, Mom, I didn't buy that for you. The twins bought it for me for Christmas. All four pitched in to cover the buck it cost. You're not the only one with underwhelming kids. I'm just sharing the joy they bring me."

There *was* real joy on her face, however, because the true gift was keeping Mom away from the white china.

Mom actually laughed. "Well, that's different. Asher didn't do much better at his age. This year he gave me a lovely silk scarf." She turned to eye Jilly. "His taste is suddenly exquisite."

"He chose it himself," Jilly said. It was technically true. She'd given him three great options so he couldn't go wrong.

Asher beamed at Jilly from his usual spot against the refrigerator. "Glad you liked it, Mom."

The golden boy's gifts had always been the very best in Mom's eyes, including the spatula set, a power drill, and even a life preserver. He stocked up on gifts while supporting fundraisers, raffles and every kid with a cause. It was hard to fault him for that, even if I received more chocolate covered almonds than even I could enjoy.

"May I ask why you called this meeting?" Mom said, staring at me over her mug. Her eyeliner was getting more dramatic by the day. I envied her steady hand but it was a bit much under the bright lights of Daisy's kitchen.

"Don't we usually have a little chat after a major incident?" I asked. "It's important to be on the same page."

"We're all on the same page," Asher said. "Chief Harper's page."

"I'm always on Kellan's page," I said. "But there are other pages we should consider."

"I'm not being lured down your path of subversion, Ivy," he said, shifting uneasily. "The chief says I'm too gullible with you."

Asher was too gullible with everyone. It was one of his key charms, though also his key weakness. No doubt that's why our deadbeat father tried to infiltrate our ranks through my brother. Asher hadn't raised the issue since our last family meeting because Jilly had told him that he could not force his agenda on the rest of us. That would help but the dam would break eventually. At least it gave me time to prepare.

"You always try to do the right thing," Mom said. "Ivy can be very wily."

"Wily! What's that supposed to mean?"

"Cunning. Crafty. Cagey, and slightly devious," Mom said. "But I prefer wily."

"I didn't need a thesaurus," I said. "I'm wondering why you're insulting the person who not only covers your rent but shares two rooms in her home."

Iris raised her hand. "Don't forget kicking in for the salon start-up, too."

"Right," I said. "Respect, Mother."

"It's a compliment," Mom said, raising her coffee in a salute. "A gift, just like this sweet mug."

Keats raced in from greeting and perhaps terrorizing my nephews' ferrets and collided with the legs of my chair. Daisy's polished floors were a hazard. His arrival reminded me to stay on track.

"Thanks for coming on short notice, everyone," I said. "I need your help."

My sisters groaned—every last one of them.

"Don't make us search for that pig," Violet said. "I'm allergic to winter."

"And I'm so clumsy," Iris said. "I might break an arm and not be able to cut hair."

"Our team could use more bodies," I said. "But if Poppy joins every day, I'll let the rest of you off the hook."

"Why target me?" Poppy said. "I work hard on the farm as it is."

"I pay well over the going rate for farmhands," I said. "But you might get a better deal over at Faraway Farm. They've got budget."

She looked at me quickly. Like the rest of the Galloway Girls, her eyes were hazel and her once colorful hair was dark brown. Our features, height and weight varied but the family resemblance was indisputable. Under the similar surface, however, we were very different. Poppy had always been sparky and rebellious. As a teen, she'd been downright mean, at least to me, the youngest. A few years of nationwide couch surfing while bouncing from one menial job to the next had eventually brought her home with a better attitude. She was still the sister most likely to set a family fire, just to see tempers flare.

After evaluating me for a second, she said, "What's that supposed to mean?"

She didn't realize I had literally thousands of HR interactions to help me read her expression and posture. Her incredibly long lashes —the best in our lineup—dropped over her eyes.

"I heard you like hanging out with the crew," I said. "And from the money they want to throw at Keats and me, you'd probably cash in over there. Plus it's an easy gig, with only a handful of animals."

Daisy put down her spray bottle and rested rubber gloves on her hips. "Ivy. As much as I hate to agree with the best mom in the world, you're being rather wily here. Certainly opaque. What's your beef with Poppy?"

As the eldest and de facto matriarch, Daisy normally solved all family disputes. Or at least did her best. It was a full-time job and she had her own fractious kids to wrangle.

"Pops," I said, "Let me ask you this. Are you aware that the TV network basically hijacked my life story to create this show? And that after failing to enlist me to consult, they're now trying to twist my arm to step into a dead woman's shoes?"

She shrugged, a master of defiance. "I don't see it the way you do. They recognized a great story and tried to get your support. It's just business."

There was a sudden stabbing pain in my chest as I realized how easily she'd throw me to the dogs. Not that I liked that metaphor. The dog shoving his ears under my dangling hand deserved better. Jilly squeezed my arm to remind me that whatever my blood family did, she was my true family.

"What am I missing here?" Daisy said, forehead furrowing. "I can't run interference if I don't know what's going on."

I took a moment to summon my cool, HR smile. "Poppy is seeing Ray Faux, the cameraman who not only let me wade into a freezing pond after his boss yesterday, but filmed it."

"I'm sure Ray didn't film it," Poppy said. "He told me he tried to help."

"He filmed it," I said. "I've seen proof. There were two camera angles and the footage had been edited into a sweet montage for the network."

Poppy's face turned bright red. That was an extremely rare phenomenon as she was typically more shameless than Mom.

"How did you see that?" Asher said.

"Like I said, they're trying to recruit me. As if seeing myself wading in there while my dog wailed his heart out on the bank would inspire me. And why would I ever want to work with people who wouldn't help? That's not my idea of a team."

Poppy glared at me, knowing I was lumping her in with the crew. "Ray could have lost his job, and he needs it."

At that moment all eyes turned to her. *On her.* Five sets of hazel, Asher's blue and Jilly's green. Even Keats sat up on his haunches to treat her to a dose of eerie blue eye. Only Percy was missing in action. The ferrets held greater allure than a fractious family meeting.

Daisy walked around the counter and crossed her arms with yellow rubber showing at each elbow. "Poppy, exactly whose side are you on?"

"There's no need to take sides," Poppy said, sliding down in her chair like a sullen teen. "I'm on everyone's team."

"You're on Team Poppy, apparently," I said, and Jilly pinched my arm.

Mom turned slowly and carefully on the stool. There was a lightness about her today that came from not being on the hot seat herself. But after watching Poppy for a few seconds, she said, "Have you fallen for this Raymond? He's only been in town a week or two. That's not how this should go, Poppy. Where's your rotation?"

We all groaned except Jilly.

"I've known him for a more than a month," Poppy said. "We met at The Tipsy Grape when they were here scouting."

"You've known about this show for a month and didn't tell me?" I felt even more violated and Keats whined.

"I didn't know what the show was about, I swear," Poppy said. "I just knew they were considering some reality thing and he made me promise not to say anything. You know what this town is like. People would have gotten in the way."

My heart still hurt and part of me wanted to believe the worst. But the clinical HR expert also saw that Poppy's long lashes were up and she met my eyes. Ray had deceived her, it seemed, more than she had deceived me.

"But you found out before the rest of us and still didn't share," Daisy said. Her brows furrowed in motherly disappointment, probably as much at her own failings as at Poppy's. There had only been so much attention to go around when we were kids and Poppy had come up short, too.

"By then I was embarrassed," she said. "I felt like I should have known. Ray was always asking me questions about my family, especially Ivy."

I pressed my lips together to keep a torrent of hot words from spilling out. Jilly helped by squeezing my arm harder, and then speaking for me. "What did you tell him?"

"Not much. That's why he kept asking." She gave me a defiant look. "I'm not a complete idiot. Have any of you ever gotten anything out of me I didn't want to share?"

"Good point," Daisy said, glancing at me. "Complete chunks of Poppy's history are missing and I have asked."

"See? Ray didn't hear anything from me that wasn't already in the public domain. Like the news or your social media following."

Mom tried again. "Are you serious about this young man, Poppy?"

The lashes came down again and it seemed like a herculean effort to raise them before answering. "No. I mean, I had hopes there for a second. He's cute. And probably the nicest guy I've dated."

"Darling, you set the bar too low," Mom said. "Some of your boyfriends have been—" She fanned imaginary stink away from her face. "Dubious. One's in jail now."

"Two," Poppy volunteered. "Best place for them. I thought Ray was a huge upgrade. It's hard to meet nice men in this town."

Iris and Violet chimed in with their agreement.

"It's really not," Mom said. "I mean in Clover Grove proper, perhaps it is. At least at your age. Most of my dates are already through their first marriage. You just need to cast your net a little wider and set your standards much higher."

Poppy shifted in obvious misery at hearing dating advice from Mom. "It's okay. I will not be trying again anytime soon."

"That's where you're wrong, Pops," I said. "You and Ray still have a future to explore."

"What?" Her mouth dropped open and her arms fell to her sides. I took some pleasure in that because it was very hard to shock Poppy, let alone make her show it. "I never want to see him again. He rolled camera on you instead of helping you yesterday. I'm... I'm ashamed over being easy to fool. I thought my creepometer had improved."

"Don't be so hard on yourself, darling," Mom said. "I married your father and that set you a terrible example."

Asher spoke at last. "Can we not go there?"

"Let's not go there," Jilly quickly agreed. "Poppy, we've all been fooled in romance before. Every last one of us. Show of hands?"

All hands rose. Daisy's was the first and she met my eyes, because I knew exactly how much she'd been fooled in the past. But I matched her quickly. When I was still in college and on the rebound from Kellan, I'd dated a string of losers before accepting no one could compare. Redirecting all my energy from romance into my career had turned me into the perfect company drone.

"Pops, we need someone on the inside now," I said. "You've shown in the past that you're a highly capable actor. So I'm asking you now to act *for* me."

She dug her palms into her eyes. "There's a word for what you're asking me to do."

"All I'm asking you to do is have a few dates. Let him do the talking."

"Be sweet and receptive," Mom said. "And feminine. He'll never know, trust me."

"I—I can't," Poppy said. "He duped me."

"Not necessarily," Jilly said. "I bet he thinks highly of you because you *haven't* cracked under his pressure to share family intel."

Poppy sat a little straighter. "Do you think?"

"I do," Jilly said. "But let me give you a full report after dinner tomorrow. I am going to cook a fabulous meal for him. A real lip-loosener. Let's see what's behind that camera."

"I don't like this," Asher said. "The chief won't, either."

"That's why you're not invited," Jilly said. "Police officers zip lips that a good meal might open." Her tone said his resistance was futile. "We'll save you some leftovers, though."

"Poppy, you can do this," I said. "I have complete faith in you. Just watch Jilly and me and follow our lead. We have powers of fakery only a decade in corporate life can give."

Mom slipped down from her stool. "That's not something to brag about, Ivy."

"Sure it is. You're probably not far wrong about my being wily. Cunning and crafty." I got up, too. "And cagey."

"Darling, you *do* realize these words also apply to your pig?" Mom said.

"Could be worse." I followed Keats to the door, where Percy was already waiting. "Wilma's one tough cookie. I'll use her as my role model."

"Again, set the bar higher," Mom said. "All of you."

CHAPTER FIFTEEN

I sent Mom back to the farm with Poppy so that Jilly and I could make a pitstop.

"For the record, I feel very uneasy about this," she said, as I turned under the Faraway Farm sign. "These people would have let you drown and made money off the footage."

"You know the old saying... keep your friends close and your enemies closer."

"Care to share the goal so that I can play my part well?"

"Goal number one is to see if Byron came home. I'm more worried about him than Wilma." Keats mumbled a response from Jilly's lap that suggested I didn't need to be too concerned about either of them. "Good to know, buddy," I said. "Then we'll focus on goal number two, which is getting a read on everyone. I wasn't at the top of my game yesterday and if Keats and Percy gave me any signs, I missed them."

"How about goals number three, four and five?" Jilly asked. "Because I bet you've got them."

"I just want to learn whatever we can about Vivian. If we can prove someone on the crew is implicated, the show will have to leave town, right?"

She nodded. "If the killer's unrelated, they'll stay and exploit the drama."

"I still think they set Wilma free on purpose and worry we won't be safe until they're gone for good." Keats whined his agreement. "See? We're targets. So while I am trying to help solve the crime, like the mayor asked, our goals are different."

Jilly smoothed her hair and pulled on her hat. Like magic, all doubt disappeared. She really was a master of the HR mask. I hoped she was right that my "face game" was just as strong. These days I felt like my powers flickered on and off like a faulty lightbulb.

Becky came out the front door before I'd even turned off the ignition. Her face was a mask, too. Someone had taken the same training we had.

"Change of heart?" she said, as Jilly and I followed Keats and Percy up the walk.

The dog stood at the bottom of the stairs and took her measure. I'd hoped for a clear sign of guilt but his posture only registered the contempt he felt for plenty of lousy people. His ears flattened but his ruff and tail didn't rise. However much I wanted her to be "the one," Keats didn't believe she was. It was possible that she was a terrific actor. Even so, he'd pick up clues.

"Yes," I said, simply. "The mayor asked me to consider the network's offer. So... I'm considering. This seemed like a good place to start doing that. Considering."

"Do you always repeat words like that?" she asked. "It makes for boring television. Maybe the network will reconsider considering you."

I offered a bright smile. "Then we'd all be happy."

"Except the mayor," Jilly said. "Who is our most important consideration, no?"

"Yes," I said. "We are responsible citizens here in Clover Grove. So the mayor's wish is our command."

Becky's fingers twitched in her pocket and I knew she was

texting the team. Moments later, Ray and Eric came out with cameras rolling.

I turned up the volume on my smile and Jilly did the same.

"Ladies," Becky said. "Those smiles are too much. It's reality TV. Look natural."

"This is natural. For us," I said. "Now, you're probably going to need warmer clothes. I noticed I wasn't the only one shivering yesterday."

"Why would we need warmer clothes?" she asked. "Chief Harper told us to stay here."

"But that didn't stop you from coming to my place yesterday. So I'm here to invite you to join our search for Wilma and Byron. Unless the dog has come home, of course."

"I don't think he's back," she said.

"You don't think so?"

She gave an impatient flick of her fingers. "We've got far bigger things to worry about than a runaway dog, Ivy."

Keats' tail did a dead drop on that statement, taking Becky's ratings with it.

"I understand that Vivian's passing is a lot to process," I said. "The case is in good hands with Chief Harper. We can't do anything to help her now, but there are animals wandering loose in the bush in winter. Them we can help."

The hand rose again, signaling the guys to stop shooting. "It's a lost cause. This whole show is a lost cause."

I glanced at Jilly and shrugged. "You're counting me out too soon, Becky. Let's get out in the bush and drum up some good footage. See what the network thinks."

"Worth a try," Ray said, nudging Becky's shoulder. "Isn't it?"

"I guess," she said. "While we get ready, why don't you run down to the barn and see if everything's still alive?"

"Be glad to," I said, through clenched teeth. Jilly hauled me around the house and when we were fully out of earshot I added, "I can stand everything else, but the contempt for animals hits me right here." I thumped my chest. "I don't know if I can follow through without doing something drastic."

"We can and we will," Jilly said. "For the animals."

I feared the worst when we arrived at the little barn. Had anyone bothered to feed and water the livestock? Clean out their stalls? I would not hesitate to have the Rescue Mafia extract them if there was one bleat of suffering.

It turned out I'd worried for nothing. The white sheep, goat, horse and hens all looked as healthy and as happy as they could in a small pen in winter. In fact, the only change was that they looked a little dirtier and more like real livestock.

The Charlie clone farm assistant came out of the barn and smiled. "Hey ladies."

"Hi there." I saw the name "Chess Cochrane" stitched into his jacket with the Faraway Farm logo. "Chess, I'm Ivy and this is Jilly. We're going out to search for my missing pig and wondered if Byron had come home."

His sad expression said it all. "That poor dog. He's so mild mannered I never expected him to bolt. They shouldn't have had him out there in the bush when he doesn't know which end is up. I've put up posters all over Clover Grove and beyond but there hasn't been a single call."

I sighed. "No one's paying attention, I'm afraid."

"Everyone is thinking about Vivian," he said. "That's understandable. But the dog—and your pig—are still alive. They deserve to be found."

"Exactly what I just told Becky. Would you like to come out to help us search?"

He shook his head. "My place is here. I'm the new Byron until the old one comes back. I hope you find him. I miss the big fella."

"We'll bring him back. He has a great coat of fur and my friends are practically experts."

"Would you mind keeping me posted?" he said.

"Of course," I said. "Thank you for caring about these animals."

"It's my job," he said. "I'd do it for free though. This goat is a hoot. I got my hands full being her playmate till Byron comes back."

"What more can you tell me about the dog?" I asked. "Anything that might help me find him."

The old man dodged just in time to avoid a head butt from the goat. "Well, he has more patience than any dog I've ever met. He may have looked low energy, just lying around and letting the goat jump on him. But one day something was in the bush and let me tell you, he grew two sizes. And the growl... I almost had to scoop up after myself." He laughed and we joined him. "Whatever it was took the hint and left. But I figured I'd been duly warned to watch my step. I have no doubt he'd put me in my place if he didn't like my work."

"Any idea what was in the bush?" I asked. "There's nothing definitive on Vivian's cause of death, but I've wondered if someone had a grudge against her."

"Dunno," Chess said. "Beyond my pay grade. They brought me in from Wyoming to wrangle this crew. I've done plenty of westerns before so this seemed like a cushy job. Byron could pretty much do it alone."

"He'd need prehensile thumbs," I said. "For the spray paint."

Chess laughed. "You noticed that, did you?"

"I hope it's not toxic."

"It's not. I made sure of it. But I've discontinued till further notice. They're not shooting down here so I figure it's okay for things to get a little dingy."

Becky bellowed from out front. "Let's go, let's go."

"Good luck to you," he said. "Hope you get the part, Ivy. If you want it."

"It would be great to work with another animal lover," I said.

Chess turned to walk back to the barn and the goat butted him repeatedly on the way.

Laughing, he turned to fend the goat off and called, "There goes my last shred of dignity."

"No dignity in farming," I said. "Spoken from experience."

"FIRST RULE OF REALITY TV?" Becky said, as we trudged through the bush after Keats. "Don't get too close to the help. They come and go and you can't get attached. Same with the livestock, come to think of it. The network is always testing testing testing. If the audience doesn't like the goat, the goat goes."

I gave her a startled look. "You don't think that's what happened with Byron, do you? Vivian called him a dud."

"I remember feeling him yank the leash out of my hand, so he left of his own accord." She gave a nasty little laugh. "Maybe he sensed his days were numbered. But I think he was too dumb for that."

Keats turned back to stare at her with his blue eye and his hackles rose.

"Becky, you know I care about animals, as do my friends." Jilly was about 20 yards behind with Edna and Gertie Rhodes. She was doing her best to keep the two older women out of camera range, because there was no telling what either of them would say or do. If I was a wild card, they were loose cannons. "It hurts when you say things like that."

"You'll have to toughen up if you want to star in this show," she said. "The network is brutal with sensitive flowers like you. They will mow you down like hay."

"Lovely. You're making a compelling case for my taking the role."

She looked around to make sure the guys were out of earshot

and then turned to me. It was the first time I noticed her eyes were green, like Jilly's, only 50 shades colder. "I don't want you to take the role. The network thinks you'd be perfect but I see a world of trouble, and I'd be the one managing you. Their values and yours collide. In this job, we don't get to make choices, you see. We do what we're told. Are you a yes-man, Ivy? I mean, honestly?"

"Well, no. We wouldn't be out here right now if I were. But as you like to remind me, my inn had a rocky start and I need money and business at Runaway Farm. I can say yes to the network for the sake of my animals."

"And your family... They're nuts."

"So right," I said. "That's a big draw for me: it would be your job to herd them."

"I didn't sign onto this show to herd cats." She sneered at Percy on my shoulder. "Even cats with big ambitions."

Percy let out a hiss. "You've been told," I said.

Becky saw that Keats was still staring at her and shuddered. "Tell him not to look at me. I don't like him."

"He's not big on you, either. But you can't always pick your colleagues."

"Yeah, I've been spoiled working with Vivian so long. We were like family." After a second she added, "When family goes right, that is."

I had to bite my lip to hold back an incredulous snort. Was this an act? Vivian had treated Becky like absolute garbage. It was possible that she had Stockholm Syndrome, where the victim starts identifying with the oppressor. That had been true of me for years at Flordale Corporation. Only my last boss had been horrible enough to make me question my beliefs, and then Keats had blown my delusions out of the water.

"Water!" Gertie called, stomping up behind us in her poncho. Under it was a camouflage parka and matching pants. The two older women had clearly been swapping fashion tips since I brought them together at Christmas.

I looked down but it just looked like regular snow to me. "What do I do?" I asked. My voice was high and squeaky and Keats froze exactly where he was. The bravest dog in the world was terrified of plunging into a pond's murky depths.

"Psych!" Gertie said, laughing. "Just wanted to hear that squeak, Ivy."

The two men had turned their cameras and caught the exchange.

"Very funny, Gertie. Maybe you could focus on finding the missing animals rather than scaring the daylights out of me."

"Wilma doesn't want to be found," she said. "Yet. When she does, she'll find us."

Edna joined us. "So now you're the pig whisperer, Gertie?"

"I've owned a few pigs in my time, old friend. You?"

"No, but I dated some," Edna said, and they both broke into a wild cackle.

Jilly and I laughed too, but Becky's mouth seemed to be locked in a pucker. If she wasn't careful it would stay that way. Or so Mom always said. She did facial exercises every night as part of her extensive bedtime self-care ritual.

"Well, pigs are smart," Gertie said. "No one gives them enough credit. And I have no doubt whatsoever that Wilma will reveal herself in due course. She's just enjoying her moment."

"But what about that food?" I asked. "Someone's been feeding her."

"There are people back here all the time. Still hoping for more treasure," she said. "No one's going to come forward and admit to it in case I shoot them. So just let the pig be."

"Not in her wiring," Edna said. "Ivy's incapable of just letting things be. Especially if that thing is an animal."

"Guilty," I said. "I won't give up till I find Wilma. And Byron.

But I'm less worried than I was about Wilma. Everyone thinks she'll be fine. Keats included."

"She will be fine," Gertie said. "Pigs are resourceful."

I sighed. "Why doesn't she want to come home? I give her the best of everything."

"It's true," Jilly said. "Ivy forfeits some good food to make sure that pig has her micronutrients."

"What Wilma really wants right now is some alone time, that's all. There are fifty animals at your farm and she's an introvert."

"You think?"

Gertie shrugged. "I think it sounds good and the cameras are rolling." She beckoned to the two men. "Over here, fellas. I've got a pig story you're going to love."

They came toward her eagerly, probably knowing that Gertie, with her long braid and a rifle concealed in her poncho, would provide great fodder for the show, if it ever did go on.

Becky followed them. "Wait, guys. I still call the shots around here."

Gertie cackled again and gave a quick flash of her rifle. "Really, girlie?"

"Yes, really. I'm the producer of Faraway Farm."

"Faraway Fart is dead in the water," Gertie said. "Oops. Did I use my hillbilly voice?"

"Gertie," I said. "Maybe we should focus on finding Byron now. That dog is not as well equipped to survive our winters as Wilma."

"Sure he is. He's bred to be outdoors year-round and he'll be fine, too." She raised her free hand in a salute. "You worry too much, Ivy."

That's when I noticed her feet were moving. Slowly but surely she was luring the crew away from Jilly and me. Edna started after them without saying a word.

All of a sudden there was a crack, followed by a scream. Becky's arms flailed as she sank into muck up to her thighs.

"Stop thrashing," Gertie said. "You'll wake the gators. They're down there hibernating under the mud."

Becky's screams grew but she did stop thrashing. "Get me out of here! Ray! Eric! Pull me out right now."

It took them a couple of minutes to find somewhere safe to put their cameras. Eric tried to offload his on me but I shook my head. "Too valuable. I'm such a klutz."

Eventually they found just the right log for the job and went back to pull their colleague from the swamp.

"Do leeches hibernate, Ivy?" Gertie called. "You seem to know a lot about animals."

I shrugged, determined not to encourage her. "Leeches are out of my bailiwick."

Freed from the mud, Becky started squelching back the way we came. "You're fired, old lady. See if you get a cameo on my show."

"Aw, boo-hoo," Gertie said. "You'll put my poncho in a knot."

Turning back, Becky crossed her arms. "I'm reporting you to the chief of police. If you did that to me, obviously you did worse to our star yesterday."

"Let the accusations fly," Gertie said. "Well, I'm always glad to see Chief Hotstuff. That's what you call him, right Edna?"

"Not on TV," Edna said, pointing at Ray, who'd picked up his camera again. "One step too far, Gertie."

It was a strange day indeed when Edna Evans was chastising someone else for taking things too far.

"This stinks," Becky yelled, like a kid having a tantrum. "It stinks!"

"It'll take a few baths but I promise it does wear off," I said. "I found out the hard way."

"You stink too," she said, walking forward again. "Everything was going great until you came along."

She continued to grumble as she sloshed away.

"Men, may I suggest you follow at a good distance," I said. "Cameras off. Give the woman her dignity."

"Not in our contract," Ray said, but he jerked his head at Eric and they did leave.

Once they were out of earshot, Gertie said, "You going to thank me now or later, Ivy?"

"Both," I said, shaking my head. "Maybe they'll think twice the next time someone is struggling. But I doubt it. Like Ray said, it's not in their contract."

We gave them a good head start and then followed. Becky's screams would have scared off the animals, had they been in earshot.

"One way or another we'll drive these people away. In the meantime, I'm sure Becky will be out of commission for your dinner party tonight."

"Ah, so there is a method to your madness," I said.

"This time." Her cackle was enough to wake those gators, both fictional and metaphorical. "Not always."

CHAPTER SIXTEEN

"I should have listened to her," I told Keats that evening, as we did our chores in the barn. "I never really gave her a fair chance."

Keats mumbled something intended to let me off the hook.

"Thank you," I said, "But it's important to take accountability for mistakes. Wilma simply wasn't my favorite animal here and she knew it. I couldn't forgive her for trying to kill me in that marsh. I bet it wasn't personal. She barely knew me by then and didn't feel safe. Maybe never did feel safe. An animal that feels safe probably doesn't want to take off." I shoved manure out the back door to add it to my pile. "If she comes home, I solemnly vow to suck up to that pig." I tossed up a shovelful too recklessly and some of the dung came back to hit me in the face. "Point taken, universe. I've already sucked up to Wilma and it didn't work. What I need to do is try something new. To figure out what makes her tick. It's not about theories of what *should* make a pig happy. She's an individual."

The next shovelful hit its mark.

"Okay, so I'm on the right track. I'll continue. I vow to understand every animal on this farm as an individual. With more than fifty, it's going to take time, but that's my job." Another shovelful landed safely. "Or at least the job I've given myself. I want every creature to feel happy and valued. Not just the ones that like me."

Percy struck me about mid-back and climbed onto my shoulder. He was perfectly capable of rocketing directly to his perch but he liked the element of suspense. Sometimes he just clung there, like a burr, and then dropped off. That was more annoying than the ascent.

"Do you know what my problem is, Percy? I'm a chronic people-pleaser. It comes from being the last of six kids. From following four girls and the golden boy. My role was to be good and quiet and hard-working. That's the only way I got attention. Then I took that attitude into my career and it sped my climb. Corporations love pleasers. Toxic corporations *exploit* pleasers."

He purred in my ear and then gave me a hard head butt. Maybe he was trying to knock that notion out of me. The very idea of pleasing and validation-seeking was foreign to cats.

"Don't worry. I'm not going to beat myself up too much. I did the best I could with what I knew at the time." The cat shifted and rebalanced as I scooped up more poop. "I left the worst of that behind in Boston but I see now that I've been seeking validation from my animals, and when my techniques failed, I either persisted or gave up. Food bribes weren't the way to Wilma's heart and I didn't try to hear her out."

I fired up another load onto the pile. "I hope I get a chance to make things right."

As Percy and I chatted, Keats did his rounds again, checking and rechecking to make sure everyone who wanted to be inside at night was locked up tight. Since Wilma vanished, he'd become hyper-diligent, almost obsessive about keeping his livestock safe. He was never a good sleeper but now he stayed at the window most of the night in constant vigilance. I wondered if Edna was still doing the same across the way.

"Buddy, let's get one thing clear," I said, when he circled back.

"There was nothing you could have done to prevent Wilma from going. Someone wanted to make a statement and they found a way. We can't be on duty 24-7. But now I have the security camera on during the day, too. And Charlie is setting up some kind of alarm." I shook my head. "I bet every passing raccoon triggers it."

Keats agreed heartily with that.

"Let's sum all this up," I said. "Keats, you and I are going to cut ourselves some slack and just do the best we can. We have over-achiever syndrome. And Percy, you're going to continue to model your nonchalance for us. How does that sound?"

Both animals chimed in at once with a yip and a meow and I laughed.

Someone else laughed, too.

I turned so fast that Percy had to dig in hard to stay seated. Keats' ruff came up and his tail went down. If I hadn't been pouring my heart out to him, he would have noticed Ray standing in the doorway, camera on his shoulder.

"Are you filming me?" I asked. "I don't remember signing any waivers." I drove the shovel hard into the manure and then put my hands on my hips. "In fact your cameras are prohibited on my property, Ray. Understood?"

"I thought you wanted to be part of the show," he said.

"If I say yes, all shooting would need to take place at Faraway Farm. I don't want my privacy invaded or my animals traumatized."

He lowered the camera. "Sorry. When you invited us for dinner I thought you were angling for a demo reel. Just trying to help out."

"Secretly shooting me discussing my failings with my pets will help me out?"

"Actually yeah. That's exactly the kind of thing the network would love."

I snapped my fingers to summon Keats and brushed past Ray to head up to the house. "But it's not the kind of thing I would love to have aired. Did it occur to you that I'm not an actor? Vivian could roll from one show to another and be someone else. I only get to be me. Forever."

He trailed after me and sighed. "I see your point, Ivy, and I'm sorry. Guess I've been in this business so long I forget how real people live." I didn't respond and eventually he added, "It's no excuse, but I don't call the shots very often. You must see that."

My umbrage faded about halfway up to the house. There was no point browbeating the man if I hoped to get information out of him. Besides, it was hypocritical. Exploitation was a two-way street tonight.

I slowed so he could catch up to us but Keats didn't settle his flags. "I overreacted, Ray, and I'm sorry. This is all so new. I've deliberately flown under the radar all my life."

"Our world has a strange set of rules and I'm not always comfortable with my job spec," he said.

"I noticed," I said. "You wanted to help me when I walked into that pond."

"Yeah, and I would have come after you no matter what if you'd lost your footing. You handle yourself well in a crisis."

"Learned the hard way, unfortunately." I stopped at the bottom of the stairs. "Did you see anything at all in the woods that day that could help us figure out what happened to Vivian?"

He shook his head. "I don't really 'see' while I'm shooting but I went over the footage several times looking for clues. It seemed like we all converged on the scene at exactly the same time. I said the same to the police when they demanded a copy."

"Any sense of who might have done this?"

"Other than your pig?" he asked. "From what I could see there was nothing but a torn glove and hoofprints."

"The town is apparently split between blaming the pig, ghosts and aliens," I said, smiling.

"And witches," he said. "I've heard that one, too."

"Not buying any of it," I said. "All my experience in HR and beyond tells me there's a human behind this tragedy."

Keats gave a mumble of agreement that startled Ray. "Did the dog just agree with you?"

I started up the stairs. "I like to think my animals understand me, but he's probably just asking for dinner. And I bet you're hungry, too."

Eric was already ensconced on the leather couch in the family room beside Poppy. Given the delicate nature of the dinner party, I'd enlisted Daisy to extract Mom for the night. There had been many a shrill protest and ultimately I'd threatened to withdraw her front suite privileges if she didn't go graciously. Mom was a good asset in some situations, but her smart mouth was a hazard. Poppy wasn't much better, but she'd been duly warned and was motivated to make things right.

Jilly poured another two whiskey sours from a tall, icy pitcher. It was my favorite cocktail. Tangy freshly squeezed lemon juice put my brain on high alert, though too much of a good thing would have the opposite effect. Her private recipe was always a hit with our gentlemen guests, which is why Jilly had chosen it. Normally she cut cocktail hour short, but tonight the pitcher tipped again and again.

By the time we adjourned to the dining room, cameras were forgotten. Poppy's normally sassy expression had been shuttered by discomfort, but she managed a stiff smile after a puckery dose of lemon. Several drinks in, however, Ray still hadn't let on that he had any special familiarity with Poppy. The way she shook out her linen napkin told me that annoyed her. And when she followed by rearranging the cutlery, I guessed it hurt, too.

Jilly dished out huge servings of her classic beef stew, a hit not only with Edna, but nearly every man alive. I dove in with gusto but Poppy just pushed a pearl onion around her plate. If Ray noticed, he didn't let on. But I think he'd stopped noticing much after the second whiskey sour.

"How are you guys doing?" Jilly asked, with a winsome smile. "We've been worried about you over there."

She was a knockout in a dress I hadn't seen since her single days in Boston. It had always been a business asset and I was pleased she'd dressed for success. I'd only managed a quick shower and change into dress pants and cashmere. Still, it felt good to remind them I wasn't always the farmer cartoon they'd imagined.

"Okay. We're okay," Ray said. "I mean, a little rattled, if I'm honest."

"Worried the killer pig will come over to finish you off, too?" I said. "Or the ghosts and aliens?"

He laughed. "None of that. I guess maybe I agree with you that a human could be behind this, and until that gets sorted none of us will feel safe."

"If it's true, wouldn't the violence be specific to Vivian?" I asked. "I heard she rubbed a few people the wrong way."

Ray shrugged. "We're in reality TV. We rub people the wrong way for a living."

"Including you, Ivy," Eric said, shoveling stew like it was his last meal. "You seemed mad enough about the show to do something drastic."

"I *was* mad. Until I realized how much good the show could do for me. For this place and my animals and my family."

Poppy flicked the pearl onion right off the plate. It rolled across the tablecloth and onto the floor. Keats was sitting watch beside me, but he certainly wasn't going to let that go to waste. I had to signal Poppy to grab it before he could. Like so many tasty things, onions were toxic.

"You mean you realized the mayor was going to make your life difficult if you didn't give in," Eric said.

This guy made Ray look like a prince. I hoped Poppy at least took solace from the fact she'd fallen for the nicer louse.

"That too," I said. "But the mayor's attention obviously meant I couldn't do anything drastic." I lifted a nice piece of beef and smiled. "Dating the chief of police makes homicide harder to pull off, too. At least I assume, having never tried."

"You don't have to try with a vicious pig," Eric said. "You can stand back and let the animals do your dirty work." He rubbed one hand over his bald head. "And it *was* dirty."

Jilly stood and served Eric a second helping of stew. "We know a little something about post-traumatic stress disorder," she said, patting his shoulder.

He flinched as if she'd sent a bolt of electricity through him.

"It's probably better to believe it's the pig," I said. "Then you know there's no malice. Vivian was in the wrong place at the wrong time with an animal that was quickly turning feral."

"But what if it wasn't?" Ray said to Eric. "Someone could come after us, too."

"Why on earth would they do that?" I asked. "You guys are just the cameramen."

"It starts at the top and trickles down," he said. "Like your dung pile."

"Then Becky would be next," Eric said. "And by that time, they'd figure it out."

"Guys, guys," Jilly said. "You're letting your thoughts run away with you. Classic signs of PTSD. I am quite sure no one wants you dead."

Ray tipped the last of the whiskey sour down his throat and then reached for his glass of wine. "You'd be wrong. We get threatened all the time by people who don't like our shows' angles."

"He's right," Eric said. "And we've done three shows and half a dozen pilots with Vivian. There's a lot of unhappy people."

"Well, Clover Grove isn't like that," I said. The words almost made me choke on a pearl onion and Keats' ears perked up hopefully. "It's truly a quaint country town."

Ray rolled his eyes. "The Langman sisters chased me with a

broom. It's the first time I've been smacked in the backside since I was a kid. There are plenty of real witches in this town."

I couldn't help laughing. "The Langmans are quite the characters."

"And the vet's wife… Beverly. Wouldn't want to meet her in dark alley."

"She has a lovely singing voice," Jilly said. "A star in our Christmas choir."

Ray got busy on his wine. "All I'm saying is that people in Clover Grove seem angry enough about the show to chase us out of town. The lady at the bookstore threatened legal action if we didn't leave."

"The network doesn't seem worried about any of that," I said.

"Like they care about the little guys," Eric said. "They'll step right over Vivian's body and keep shooting with you because ratings were good on the premiere."

"I did expect them to be more upset about losing their star. They have a long history with her."

Lifting his linen napkin, Ray patted his forehead. His arty swoop of hair was limp with sweat. "She was making too many demands. There were meetings on meetings."

"And yelling," Eric added.

"When you're successful, it's normal to want more," I said.

"Not *that* much more. She tripled her salary request for this show. Like it was a tough gig."

I laughed again. "She knew something about farming and it is a tough gig. She would have ended up covered in manure. She deserved more money."

"She was a—"

"Ray," Eric said. "Zip it."

Ray made a point of looking around. "I don't see any cameras rolling, Eric. If I say Vivian rode a broom, no one can prove it."

"It's okay," I said. "We understand completely. Jilly and I come from a very cutthroat background."

"Both of us were bullied," Jilly said. "A lot."

"That's why I had zero tolerance for it when I was a manager. It was tough to enforce though. I could never get men to report it. Pride, I guess."

Ray and Eric glanced at each other sheepishly. No matter how tipsy, their pride wouldn't let them report it now. But their look said it all.

"Since there's no camera rolling, I'll admit I'm not broken up over seeing the last of Vivian," Ray said. "I really wanted to see her turfed and humiliated. Becky too."

He sat back suddenly and pressed his lips together. Eric did, too. The atmosphere changed and I knew the information highway had been closed for traffic.

"More stew?" Jilly asked.

"No thanks," Ray said. "It was amazing, but we've got to get back to our farm and see how things are going."

Our farm... The words sent a shot of annoyance through me.

"Becky is probably nervous alone," I said.

"Your killer pig would have its work cut out taking her down," Eric said, bringing the conversation full circle to Wilma's supposed guilt. "She's a fighter. We admire that."

"Of course," I said, getting up to walk them to the door with Jilly. Poppy didn't follow and Ray just gave her a sloppy nod. We waited with them till the cab arrived and helped them load the cameras safely. Keats kept tight herding maneuvers until they were inside the vehicle, even going so far as to jab Ray repeatedly in the shin with his nose. He didn't seem to notice.

After they drove off, Jilly said, "Either one of them could have done it. They both feel pretty burned."

"Becky too," I said. "We've seen how internal politics can erode people till they're desperate. The big question is, did someone act alone or were they in on it together?"

By the time we got back to the family room, my sister was curled up with Percy on the couch. The cat was kneading her sweater gently and I could hear the comforting purr from yards away.

"That meal was delicious, Jilly," Poppy said. "But I don't think I'll ever eat stew again."

"You will, Pops," I said, signaling Keats to join them. This was clearly a job for two pets. "Just wait till the right pearl onion comes along."

Percy delivered a head butt that was harder than necessary.

"One concussion was enough, thank you very much, Percy. I'm thinking as fast as my neurons will fire." A few more yards brought the answer. "The old barn. She said there was an old barn back here where her dad hid a neglected cow and calf belonging to the Swensons. He was one of the original rescuers. But when old Frank found out, the Kinkaids weren't safe here anymore."

Keats turned to give me the full benefit of both eyes. Bingo!

"Okay, it sounds like Wilma may have taken refuge in this old barn. Now that would be one smart pig, Keats."

He gave a grumble and moved faster.

"And one brilliant dog for figuring that out. Let's get her."

I picked up my boots and hurried, knowing there was an end to this everlasting forest. One day the township would buy up this land and turn it into subdivisions, I supposed. At least if Faraway Farm brought the glory the mayor hoped.

It may have been 10 minutes but felt like an hour before we finally saw a glimpse of red through the trees. Sure enough, there was a very old, dilapidated barn.

"Seriously? This wreck is preferable to the stellar accommodations at my farm? Wilma must hate us if she's chosen to shack up here."

When we got a little closer, however, I realized Wilma may not have made the choice at all. The only thing new about this place was the portable fencing surrounding it. Had the Pefferlaws stolen my pig? That didn't seem like the homesteader way. Many kept communal henhouses and gardens. Sharing is caring, some said.

"Wilma?" I called. "Are you there?"

The barn door was hanging loose and there was a white plastic fence across the opening. After a few minutes, my big pig ambled into view.

From where I stood she looked fine. Better than fine. She came as close to smiling as that pig ever had. The food must be very good here, because the company obviously wasn't.

But that's where I was wrong.

Wilma finally had company she liked.

CHAPTER EIGHTEEN

A taller, fluffier shape stepped into the frame of the doorway. "Byron! You're here!"

I was thrilled to see the two animals together and in good health. They stood side by side staring at us placidly. Neither seemed at all anxious for help.

"What is going on here? Did you two elope to be together?" I started walking around the perimeter to find a way in. "It wasn't necessary. I'm open to any kind of arrangement you want. Byron, my farm is your farm."

Keats gave a sharp bark in reproof. Nearly all animals were welcome in our ark, but apparently not other dogs. Or maybe just bigger, tougher dogs.

"We need to welcome him if they're happy together," I said. "I won't stand in the way of Wilma's happiness." After a minute I added, "Of course I will need to work things out with the show, but they haven't put much effort into looking for Byron."

Keats grumbled as he followed me along the fence and when I found a spot where the plastic panels overlapped, he stopped me from going in.

"What?" I stared around and then it hit me. "Someone deliberately trapped these animals here and everyone in a fifty-mile radius probably knows I've lost my pig. Ergo... we've got a problem."

Keats' tail signaled trouble indeed. It wasn't an immediate threat because otherwise he'd be puffed and growling. But that didn't mean we wouldn't run into the pignapper on the way back through that bush.

"I can't leave them here. But I don't want to face the pignapper alone and put you and Percy at risk. So, here's what we're going to do. We'll call Gertie and her rifle for backup. I bet she knows a faster way in here and I wouldn't put it past her to march into Finch and Starling's living room if necessary. In the meantime, we're going to start herding these two back to Gertie's house until she meets up with us. And by 'we,' I mean you."

He let out a huff of disgust that Percy echoed.

"Unless either one of you has a better plan, I'm going in."

There were no mumbles or meows so I took that as reluctant agreement.

"Okay, but you two had better stay out here. I don't trust either of them."

Keats whined but I stood firm. He was smaller than the coyotes Byron was bred to kill.

After leaving a message for Gertie, I pulled the fence aside, walked into the pen and closed the opening behind me. Byron barked once. It was deep, menacing and protective of his herd of one.

"Byron, you know us. I've watched you play with your little goat baby."

I advanced slowly and his tail came up equally slowly.

"I can see you've been taking good care of my girl, Wilma. She seems besotted with you. How do I know? She hasn't mowed you down. And I think—it's really hard to be sure—but I think she's gazing at you."

Keats whined to tell me to get a move on it.

"Right. Business. I've got to get these two home and I'm not sure how to go about it."

I pulled the second gate aside, expecting them to charge into the pen area. They didn't. Instead, Byron moved in front of Wilma and backed her further into the old barn.

"Don't you want to come out? What's the appeal in this old dump?" I turned on my phone light and peered inside. "Ah. I see. Plenty of food and bedding. Your captors have at least taken good care of you."

I signaled Keats and Percy to stay back in case the big dog decided to take issue with them. Then I eased around the two big animals carefully. Keats did as I asked, but naturally Percy ignored me. He jumped over the first gate and the second and slipped right through my feet to run ahead with his tail up.

The barn was in better shape than it looked from the outside. The walls were sound and the roof okay, at least with a heavy coating of snow. It was probably warm enough with two bodies inside, despite the broken door.

"Okay folks, let's go," I said. "Take a last look at your sweet retreat because it's back to real life for you."

I flicked the light into the back to make sure no animal was left behind. In one of the corners a tarp lay in a heap on the floor. Walking over, I nudged the material aside with my boot.

Underneath lay a small shovel. I would have assumed it was for mucking out, but all the muck was still here. It was a bit ripe inside from big and bigger poop.

Percy stepped lightly over the tarp and then started scraping invisible kitty litter over the silver metal.

Silver metal with rust along its edge.

Dark rust that had... dribbled?

"Oh," I said, dropping the tarp and backing away. I turned, and then turned back. Outside, Keats' whining escalated to a sharp yelp.

"It's okay, buddy," I called, although it was so *not* okay. "What do I do? I can't just leave it here. What if it's gone by the time the police arrive?" I bent over and carefully scooped up the shovel, careful to keep it wrapped in the tarp. "How am I going to handle all this and the animals?"

I took another look around, scanning again and again. There was something else... I felt it. And Percy, who was now scaling the wall to reach the rafters, apparently agreed. I was impressed with his athleticism and let him do his thing while I urged the big dog and the pig to go outside.

Neither one budged. Stockholm syndrome struck again.

"Wilma, please," I said. "I know we've had our differences, but I want you back at Runaway Farm. You are very special to me and I'm sorry if I haven't always shown that. I'm willing to hear you on whatever changes you'd like to make to your living arrangements."

She still didn't move, so I tucked the tarp under my arm, took a huge risk and knelt in front of her. Staring into her piggy eyes, I said, "Please come home."

The pig was an immovable force. She didn't even blink.

Standing, I turned and tried another tack. "Byron, or whatever your name was before the show gave you a new one, I need your help. Wilma belongs at Runaway Farm, not stuck out in the bush. And you do, too. That TV set is not a home and they don't value your breed for what it is. And frankly, I could use a dog like you."

There was another yelp outside and it sounded indignant.

"I've got some big personalities at my farm and with all the new additions—and the freelance gigs we take on—there's too much work to go around. If you could take over Drama Llama and the thugs, as well as keeping Wilma happy, I would be honored to have you forever."

Whether or not I got through to him, or he just decided it was time to move, was hard to say. Either way, the big dog started walking and when he did, Wilma followed like a meek kitten.

Meanwhile, my not-so-meek kitten was up in the rafters yowling

CHAPTER SEVENTEEN

The next morning I headed out to Gertie's alone.

Well, I was never alone with Keats and Percy, of course, but I'd asked the Mafia to take the day off. Cori Hogan and the main crew had put in long hard hours hunting for a pig who didn't want to be found. I suspected Gertie was right about that, and I also had faith that Wilma would turn up when she was good and ready. That didn't mean I wanted to stop looking, but I did want to give all the volunteers a day off. At least 20 people had joined the hunt yesterday and no one had found so much as a hoofprint.

"Is she still out here, buddy?" I asked the dog as he trotted along just ahead of me. "Can you sense her? How about Byron?"

He looked back with his blue eye and grumbled something cheeky.

"Fine. I don't suppose you'd waste your time on a lost cause. You'd be leading me down a different path."

The happy pant served as a nod. Exactly.

"But Gertie says she and Edna covered her entire property yesterday, while Cori and the rest took on the Swenson property. They came up empty." Keats was moving fast and I had to hurry to keep up. "Will you take it easy, please? If I break a leg or we fall in a secret swamp this will not go well for you."

He slowed a little and made a circle around me, either to be rude or to rush me.

"Not a sheep, Keats. Not a goat. I'm fully capable of going on strike."

Percy added to my protest with an exasperated yowl. His legs were much shorter than ours and the deep snow made for heavy going.

"Climb up, Percy," I said. "I should have brought your carrier. Keats didn't let on we'd be taking a major expedition."

Once the cat was settled on my shoulder we resumed trekking.

"If we find her, what am I going to do? I have rope in my backpack but I can't lasso her. Even Edna couldn't rope her. I'm going to have to rely on her goodwill."

Keats panted a ha-ha-ha.

"Yes, she's a grumpy pig but we're turning over a new leaf, remember? I am going to woo this pig not with food bribes, but understanding. There's gotta be something that motivates her and I will find it. She's not happy with her life at Runaway Farm and we both need to do something about it."

He yipped a protest, evidently standing behind his own performance as farm manager.

"I don't buy it," I said. "You take more dives at her than the other animals and I bet they're not all necessary."

He yipped again, more shrilly.

"I'm not saying you're a bully. Only *you* know that. It's more that we both got burned by her and we put up a wall to make sure it didn't happen again." I stared around at what seemed like never-ending trees, a blend of leafless deciduous and bushy coniferous of every variety. In summer, this area would be impenetrable. "We need to open our hearts to Wilma. I know you're just trying to protect me but we've got to give pigs a chance. Everyone deserves that."

His fluffy tail drooped a little. He wanted to run the farm his way and normally I let him. But with my new mission to dig deep with all of the animals, we'd need to tailor our approach. Even the chickens had their own personalities. I couldn't indulge every feathered whim but I could do better.

Keats gave me a questioning look and I shrugged. "Right. It's not like I have a lot of time on my hands, but Poppy wants more hours. I'll let her do some of the routine work while I focus on the specialized tasks. Namely communing with the livestock and manure management." He panted a laugh and I joined in. "The latter keeps me out of trouble." I stumbled over a log, spun my arms and then squealed as Percy dug in to regain his balance. "Well, more trouble."

Keats herded me into an easier "lane" and I decided to let him drive. Sometimes it was nice to gear down and be a sheep and a follower. I didn't have that luxury often.

"Do you know where we're going?" I asked. "Because you don't even seem to be searching."

The dog surged out in front and his white tuft gave an authoritative swish. As a sheep, I would apparently only receive information on a need-to-know basis.

"In my humble opinion, I do need to know," I said. "Am I walking all the way to Dorset Hills? Because I should probably let Jilly know my whereabouts."

He kept right on trotting.

Slowing, I got out my phone to check our coordinates. It felt like we'd walked miles... because we had walked miles. More if you counted the level of difficulty.

"Looks like we're close to the Pefferlaws' property line," I said. "I know it's even rougher terrain than Gertie's, and I don't love the idea of us being here on our own. If you think Wilma's out this way how about we round up a team and come back later?"

He still kept right on trotting.

"Keats! I can see that you've locked onto a target and are ignoring your herd, but sheep are people, too."

He turned with a blue-eyed stare that practically barked "duh."

"That is no way to lead, buddy. I'm sending you for more training at Ordeal School."

Percy gave an odd little meow in my ear. It wasn't part of his usual vocal repertoire.

Think, he seemed to be saying. Think.

"Ah, so that's why I'm being treated like a particularly dense sheep? Do I already know the answer?"

Percy gave a purr-meow that was used only on special occasions, generally to urge me toward the cupboard containing the cat treats.

I spun right around to check our surroundings. Still I saw nothing but trees—the same trees, only different. The only difference, I supposed, was that these belonged to the Pefferlaws. The couple had arrived early in the homesteading rush and snapped up the land at a bargain price. Real estate had skyrocketed since then, especially for such a big property, so they'd done well.

"I've never crossed paths with Finch and Starling," I said. "Which is odd, considering how many community events I've attended lately. Finch and Starling sound like made-up homesteader names, don't they? I bet it's more like Reginald and Constance."

Keats granted me a laugh and kept on trucking.

Something twinkled in my memory and I tried to catch a glimpse of it. "Who owned this land before the homesteader birds? I think I know this. Percy?"

A purr-meow egged me on.

"Someone mentioned this recently. Around Christmas. Ah! I've got it. Martha Kinkaid! She told me her family basically got forced off this land during the feuding between the Swenson and Milloy families. They moved into town and boarded their livestock at Runaway Farm."

Percy delivered a head butt that was harder than necessary.

"One concussion was enough, thank you very much, Percy. I'm thinking as fast as my neurons will fire." A few more yards brought the answer. "The old barn. She said there was an old barn back here where her dad hid a neglected cow and calf belonging to the Swensons. He was one of the original rescuers. But when old Frank found out, the Kinkaids weren't safe here anymore."

Keats turned to give me the full benefit of both eyes. Bingo!

"Okay, it sounds like Wilma may have taken refuge in this old barn. Now that would be one smart pig, Keats."

He gave a grumble and moved faster.

"And one brilliant dog for figuring that out. Let's get her."

I picked up my boots and hurried, knowing there was an end to this everlasting forest. One day the township would buy up this land and turn it into subdivisions, I supposed. At least if Faraway Farm brought the glory the mayor hoped.

It may have been 10 minutes but felt like an hour before we finally saw a glimpse of red through the trees. Sure enough, there was a very old, dilapidated barn.

"Seriously? This wreck is preferable to the stellar accommodations at my farm? Wilma must hate us if she's chosen to shack up here."

When we got a little closer, however, I realized Wilma may not have made the choice at all. The only thing new about this place was the portable fencing surrounding it. Had the Pefferlaws stolen my pig? That didn't seem like the homesteader way. Many kept communal henhouses and gardens. Sharing is caring, some said.

"Wilma?" I called. "Are you there?"

The barn door was hanging loose and there was a white plastic fence across the opening. After a few minutes, my big pig ambled into view.

From where I stood she looked fine. Better than fine. She came as close to smiling as that pig ever had. The food must be very good here, because the company obviously wasn't.

But that's where I was wrong.

Wilma finally had company she liked.

A taller, fluffier shape stepped into the frame of the doorway. "Byron! You're here!"

I was thrilled to see the two animals together and in good health. They stood side by side staring at us placidly. Neither seemed at all anxious for help.

"What is going on here? Did you two elope to be together?" I started walking around the perimeter to find a way in. "It wasn't necessary. I'm open to any kind of arrangement you want. Byron, my farm is your farm."

Keats gave a sharp bark in reproof. Nearly all animals were welcome in our ark, but apparently not other dogs. Or maybe just bigger, tougher dogs.

"We need to welcome him if they're happy together," I said. "I won't stand in the way of Wilma's happiness." After a minute I added, "Of course I will need to work things out with the show, but they haven't put much effort into looking for Byron."

Keats grumbled as he followed me along the fence and when I found a spot where the plastic panels overlapped, he stopped me from going in.

"What?" I stared around and then it hit me. "Someone deliberately trapped these animals here and everyone in a fifty-mile radius probably knows I've lost my pig. Ergo... we've got a problem."

Keats' tail signaled trouble indeed. It wasn't an immediate threat because otherwise he'd be puffed and growling. But that didn't mean we wouldn't run into the pignapper on the way back through that bush.

"I can't leave them here. But I don't want to face the pignapper alone and put you and Percy at risk. So, here's what we're going to do. We'll call Gertie and her rifle for backup. I bet she knows a faster way in here and I wouldn't put it past her to march into Finch and Starling's living room if necessary. In the meantime, we're going to start herding these two back to Gertie's house until she meets up with us. And by 'we,' I mean you."

He let out a huff of disgust that Percy echoed.

"Unless either one of you has a better plan, I'm going in."

There were no mumbles or meows so I took that as reluctant agreement.

"Okay, but you two had better stay out here. I don't trust either of them."

Keats whined but I stood firm. He was smaller than the coyotes Byron was bred to kill.

After leaving a message for Gertie, I pulled the fence aside, walked into the pen and closed the opening behind me. Byron barked once. It was deep, menacing and protective of his herd of one.

"Byron, you know us. I've watched you play with your little goat baby."

I advanced slowly and his tail came up equally slowly.

"I can see you've been taking good care of my girl, Wilma. She seems besotted with you. How do I know? She hasn't mowed you down. And I think—it's really hard to be sure—but I think she's gazing at you."

Keats whined to tell me to get a move on it.

"Right. Business. I've got to get these two home and I'm not sure how to go about it."

I pulled the second gate aside, expecting them to charge into the pen area. They didn't. Instead, Byron moved in front of Wilma and backed her further into the old barn.

"Don't you want to come out? What's the appeal in this old dump?" I turned on my phone light and peered inside. "Ah. I see. Plenty of food and bedding. Your captors have at least taken good care of you."

I signaled Keats and Percy to stay back in case the big dog decided to take issue with them. Then I eased around the two big animals carefully. Keats did as I asked, but naturally Percy ignored me. He jumped over the first gate and the second and slipped right through my feet to run ahead with his tail up.

The barn was in better shape than it looked from the outside. The walls were sound and the roof okay, at least with a heavy coating of snow. It was probably warm enough with two bodies inside, despite the broken door.

"Okay folks, let's go," I said. "Take a last look at your sweet retreat because it's back to real life for you."

I flicked the light into the back to make sure no animal was left behind. In one of the corners a tarp lay in a heap on the floor. Walking over, I nudged the material aside with my boot.

Underneath lay a small shovel. I would have assumed it was for mucking out, but all the muck was still here. It was a bit ripe inside from big and bigger poop.

Percy stepped lightly over the tarp and then started scraping invisible kitty litter over the silver metal.

Silver metal with rust along its edge.

Dark rust that had... dribbled?

"Oh," I said, dropping the tarp and backing away. I turned, and then turned back. Outside, Keats' whining escalated to a sharp yelp.

"It's okay, buddy," I called, although it was so *not* okay. "What do I do? I can't just leave it here. What if it's gone by the time the police arrive?" I bent over and carefully scooped up the shovel, careful to keep it wrapped in the tarp. "How am I going to handle all this and the animals?"

I took another look around, scanning again and again. There was something else... I felt it. And Percy, who was now scaling the wall to reach the rafters, apparently agreed. I was impressed with his athleticism and let him do his thing while I urged the big dog and the pig to go outside.

Neither one budged. Stockholm syndrome struck again.

"Wilma, please," I said. "I know we've had our differences, but I want you back at Runaway Farm. You are very special to me and I'm sorry if I haven't always shown that. I'm willing to hear you on whatever changes you'd like to make to your living arrangements."

She still didn't move, so I tucked the tarp under my arm, took a huge risk and knelt in front of her. Staring into her piggy eyes, I said, "Please come home."

The pig was an immovable force. She didn't even blink.

Standing, I turned and tried another tack. "Byron, or whatever your name was before the show gave you a new one, I need your help. Wilma belongs at Runaway Farm, not stuck out in the bush. And you do, too. That TV set is not a home and they don't value your breed for what it is. And frankly, I could use a dog like you."

There was another yelp outside and it sounded indignant.

"I've got some big personalities at my farm and with all the new additions—and the freelance gigs we take on—there's too much work to go around. If you could take over Drama Llama and the thugs, as well as keeping Wilma happy, I would be honored to have you forever."

Whether or not I got through to him, or he just decided it was time to move, was hard to say. Either way, the big dog started walking and when he did, Wilma followed like a meek kitten.

Meanwhile, my not-so-meek kitten was up in the rafters yowling at me but I couldn't turn back now. The smaller ship was sailing back to the ark and I wanted to stay afloat.

"Percy, leave it," I called. "We'll come back, I promise."

Keats gave me a baleful look as the big dog passed without so much as acknowledging his existence. Clearly I'd misjudged the threat to my greatest asset.

"I'm so sorry, buddy. I was afraid he'd lump you in with the coyotes. But now you can bring everyone home. You guide Byron while he guides Wilma. Got it?"

Keats mumbled a surly confirmation and I pulled the gate aside.

"Please, boys, don't let Wilma slip away. I know she likes you, Byron, but she's a fickle beast. I'm afraid this was just a convenient fling because you were trapped together."

Percy took the lead, Byron followed the cat, and Keats came behind, slashing back and forth in an arc. I came last, cradling the shovel and trying not to think about what it meant or how it got there. A shudder racked me anyway. If this had been used two days ago to shove Vivian into the pond, then someone would undoubtedly reclaim it at some point. If that happened while my parade was in progress, I stood to lose some or all of the participants.

Keats stopped and went into a point while the others kept rolling.

"What is it?" My heart kicked up even more. "The shovel owner?"

Cocking his head, Keats evaluated and then dismissed the threat. As he loped after the others, I heard the roar of a vehicle. It couldn't be the killer or Keats wouldn't leave me.

"It must be Gertie on her ATV," I said. "Bad idea in these conditions. She could get thrown."

She hurtled into sight, long braid lifting and curling like a heavy snake under her helmet. Her ride today wasn't an ATV, however. It was a sleek red snowmobile.

My throat tightened as I pictured the animals scattering. Gertie slowed to a crawl, however, and Wilma continued to move along nicely.

"Hop on," Gertie yelled over the motor. "Let's get this crew to hustle."

I did as she said, balancing the shovel in the tarp between us. Percy left his place in the lead and jumped onto my shoulder.

"Don't go too fast, please," I said, "Or Percy will fly off."

"Not too fast, not too slow," she said, turning. "Here, hold this, will you?"

She tried to pass me her rifle but I demurred. "Keep it, Gertie. There's a chance you might need it."

"At your service." Revving the machine, she moved out in front and said, "Hit it, Byron. And you hold the line, Keats. There are plenty of sardines at my place for everyone."

Circling like a skilled cowhand, she helped drive everyone slowly, surely and safely back through the bush. Finally we passed under the arch into her yard and sent the animals into the barn.

Another snowmobile sat off to one side, covered in snow. A hint of blue paint showed through.

"His and hers," she said. "Saul loved hitting the skidoo trails in winter but I never had the heart after he passed. Glad they still run."

"Thank you, Gertie," I said, as she closed the barn door and latched it. "I hope you don't mind if I invite Chief Harper over for a chat. Plus Charlie's coming with the trailer to pick up Wilma and Byron."

Pulling off her helmet, she smoothed her gray hair, right to the end of her long braid. "Always glad to see Chief Hotstuff," she said, letting Keats and Percy escort us to the house. "And Charlie Forbes is a fine man. Much too good for your mother's stable of fools."

I laughed as I followed her inside. "I've told him so myself, but there's no accounting for taste. Wilma's fallen for Byron, for example."

"Well, he's a handsome dog, no question about that. He also has a good head on his shoulders. I can't imagine the last month has been easy for him with that crew and getting loose in the woods."

As she put on the kettle, I sat at the kitchen table, carefully settling the tarp-wrapped shovel at my feet.

"That old barn belonged to the Kinkaid family, right?" I said. "Martha mentioned it when we were talking about the Swenson-Milloy feud."

Gertie nodded, pulling a couple of packets of instant cocoa out of the cupboard, plus half a dozen tins of the promised sardines. "Haven't thought about it, let alone seen it, for years. The Pefferlaws aren't particularly warm so Saul and I kept to our side of the divide."

"I've never met them," I said. "Can you think of any reason they'd steal Wilma and Byron? Someone had set up a pen to hold them hostage."

"Finch and Starling are quirky," Gertie said, twisting the key of a sardine tin. "I mean, the names say it all, right? Birdbrains."

I laughed. "I figured those were just their homesteader names."

"Exactly. They're private, which I understand, but I get a bad vibe from them." The electric kettle switched off and she peered at me through a cloud of steam as she poured water into the cocoa. "I'm hardly one to judge when I take pride in my own eccentricity." Stirring the cocoa, she added, "I wasn't always that way, though."

"You were put in an awkward situation with all those treasure hunters," I said. "Maybe the Pefferlaws struggled with that, too. But I still don't see what they'd want with my pig."

She set the mug of cocoa in front of me and perched on the chair opposite. "That reality TV show has a lot of people rattled. They sent their cameras everywhere, scouting. People with something to hide were scared." Taking a sip, she fanned her mouth. "Minnie and I didn't have much of a reputation to lose."

I tried to sip the scalding cocoa and failed. "Minnie?"

"My rifle. My best friend. Becky and her minions beat it out of here pretty fast when I introduced her."

"So you're thinking that Finch and Starling may have tried to undermine the show by stealing the production's dog and the pig from the farm that inspired it?"

"There's only one way to find out," she said. "After we get rid of the chief, how about you, Minnie and I take a drive?"

CHAPTER NINETEEN

Gertie didn't mind that Keats stood on her poncho while we drove over to see the Pefferlaws later. I felt less welcoming of her pet, Minnie. The rifle sat at her feet, and she had shoved the seat back to make room for it.

"Is he always that supercilious?" she asked.

"Supercilious? Kellan? No, you know that." I thought about it for a second. "Only when he's annoyed at me for putting myself—and others—in danger."

"Sure, he is. Mr. Haughty McSnobalot."

The voice came from the back seat and I turned to toss Edna Evans what I hoped was a withering stare. The problem with being a blank face expert is that I didn't have a vast repertoire of expressions to draw on in situations like this.

"He has good reason to be worried about my wandering out in the bush, Edna. Turns out there's a shovel-wielding murderer around."

"Who happens to be down one shovel right now," Edna said. "Good thing I showed up when I did. Here I thought Gertie and I would just shoot some tin cans and I find you're off on an adventure.

Without me. A card-carrying member of your dream team. Who's just happened to save your life a few times."

"It wasn't deliberate," I said. "Jilly isn't here either and she predates you."

"Fine. I take back my comment about Kellan. Or maybe not. He's always snooty with me."

I continued to direct some withering into the rearview mirror and ended up stalling the truck.

"Edna. You know better than to disparage my boyfriend. People get fired for less."

"You'll have to settle for giving me whiplash," she said. "Super-cilious. Disparage. What's with the big words, ladies? Are you trying to outclass me? Because I've got an arsenal of those, too. But I try to keep it simple."

She thumped the back of the passenger seat—the throne she now considered rightfully hers. Gertie hadn't consulted and it was hard to argue with Minnie. At least Edna had left her gun at the house. I wondered what the cab driver had thought as he ferried her there in her camouflage outfit accessorized with a suspiciously large kit bag that rattled with empty baked bean cans. No wonder she'd been declining meal service from Jilly lately. The air in here might just get a little sour.

I turned the key again. "How about we all do a restart so that we can be conciliatory with the Pefferlaws? How about that word, Edna?"

"Nice would work just as well," she said.

"And be just as unlikely," Gertie said. "Edna and I don't do nice. We shoot up bean cans and long for better targets."

Both women chuckled and peace was restored.

"I'm sure Finch and Starling have more delicate sensibilities," I said.

"Hippies," Gertie said. "They try to live off the grid."

"Flower children," Edna added. "There will be tie-dye."

"Live and let live," I said. "I'm basically a homesteader myself on a larger scale. People in glass inns can't throw stones."

"No, but we can," Gertie said. "Edna and I remember a time when this town had common sense."

"And culture," Edna added. "I fully supported the Clover Grove Culture Revival Project. What's happened to that, Ivy?"

"Temporarily derailed by Faraway Farm," I said. "The mayor's interest in supporting us flagged when showbiz came knocking."

"Typical politician," Gertie said. "More concerned about cash than quality."

"I like Meryl," I said. "She's a good aunt to Bronwen and that goes far in my books. But she does seem a little blinded by the spotlight." I turned into the Pefferlaws' lane. "I suppose she thinks she's doing the best for this town."

No one answered the door of the farmhouse when we knocked. I snapped a photo with my phone to show Martha Kinkaid later. I visited her often at Sunny Acres Retirement Villa, which had done much to cleanse bad memories from the place. Keats and Percy pretty much had free run and they brought a lot of smiles to the residents.

"Hey! What do you think you're doing?"

We turned and I felt Minnie twitch against my back. A dark-haired man came up behind us with a short-haired brindle dog that was almost as large as Byron and far more fearsome. Keats' signals all shot into the red zone and I didn't blame him when I saw the dog's fangs.

"Well, hi there," I said. "I'm Ivy Galloway and you probably know Gertie Rhodes and Edna Evans." Bending, I picked up Percy and popped him onto my shoulder for safety. "This is Percy and my sheepdog is Keats."

"That's about fifty words too many considering you didn't

answer my question," he said. "Why are you taking pictures of my house?"

I amped up the mollifying smile. This was one hostile home-steader and it didn't take much to rile my companions. At least the human ones. "I'm a friend of Martha Kinkaid, whose family built this house. I thought she'd like to see a photo, that's all." I made a show of looking around. "You've kept it up so beautifully."

"Spoken like a greasy politician," he said. "I expect you'll run for office someday."

"What a terrible thing to say, Finch Pefferlaw," Gertie said, trying to step in front of me. "You've met me and you've met Edna Evans. Do you really think we'd be friends with someone like that? Or would we be more likely to shoot them? Use your head."

"I don't know what's what anymore," he said. "People in this town aren't what they seem."

His wife joined him. She was as fair as he was dark but her expression was equally unfriendly. Their parkas and boots were from the workwear supplier in town, just like mine. There was no tie-dye that I could see. It was somewhat disappointing.

"That's true everywhere," I said. "I spent ten years in Boston working in HR. No one is what they seem."

"I am," Gertie said. "I'm exactly as crazy as I seem."

"Me too," Edna said.

I laughed and shook my head. "You're not, though. That's just the thing. Finch is right."

"Agreeing with me won't get you anywhere," he said. "It's a polit-ical manipulation. Right, Starling?"

"Where is this political business coming from?" I asked. "I'm a small farmer, just like you."

His wife snorted. "You're not just like us, and saying so proves his point. You're just a pretend farmer in a fancy inn, who has Holly-wood falling all over her."

"Ah. You're mistaking Faraway Farm for my own," I said. "Whereas I see myself as an innocent victim."

"Don't we all," Edna said. "My rep has little basis in reality."

Finch was not to be sidetracked. "We heard the mayor is pushing hard for you to take over that show."

"After the star was killed practically on our land," Starling added. "Everyone thinks your pig did it, but we think you did. People seem to drop like flies around you and you have the most to gain."

I felt Minnie pressing against my spine but I had plenty of backbone without the rifle's help.

"It's so interesting that you should say that, when I wondered if *you* might be the killers."

"Us!" Finch took a step forward with the dog, whose lip curled to show even more fang. The rolling growl made Keats sound like a pussycat.

"How dare you?" Starling said. "We live a simple life without any of the modern conveniences of corruption."

"Well, you seem pretty tuned in for folks off the grid," Edna said.

"We visit the co-op and the feedstore," Finch said. "We hear things. No one's saying we did anything wrong, whereas plenty of people say Ivy did."

"Some people are saying you stole my pig," I said. "Other people are saying you stole the show's dog. And I'm saying I found them in your old barn today."

Finch turned an ugly shade of red. Living off the grid wasn't keeping his blood pressure down. "That's a lie!"

"Good thing I got photos," I said. "Which I shared with the police, who are probably out there now."

"They can't come on my property without permission."

I shrugged. "I would imagine they knocked like I did. Might even have a warrant. I didn't ask."

"A warrant?" Starling said. "Why? Livestock run off all the time."

"That's what I said, but no one sides with me."

"Get out of here, all of you," Finch said. "Or I'll set the dog on you."

"Do that and I'll set Minnie on you," Gertie said. "Would you like to meet her?"

Starling pulled Finch back by his sleeve. "Just let them go. It's all poppycock."

"Poppycock," Gertie said. "I've always liked that word."

"Or claptrap," Edna said.

"Rubbish is good, too," I said. "But to get back to the point, I wanted to let you know that I rescued the animals and took a good look around. I thank you for not abusing them at least. Wilma seemed quite happy about her vacation."

Finch and Starling stared at each other and then turned without another word and walked into the bush together.

"Well," Edna said, beating Gertie to the truck and pulling open the passenger door. "I guess Ivy was right about jumping to conclusions. They're not peaceniks at all."

Gertie slid Minnie into the rear footwell and climbed into the back seat. "I vote for renaming them Falcon and Buzzard."

Keats settled on Edna's lap and gave a pant of relief, while Percy settled in Gertie's.

"They're some of the most belligerent people I've met in Clover Grove," I said.

"Negative people take such a toll on my mood," Gertie said. "Let's go shoot some bean cans and cheer up, Edna."

"You got it. And I'd like to do some preparedness planning with you, after getting a closer look at your neighbors. When the end comes, danger will be close at hand."

"Never fear," Gertie said. "Those birds may survive without TV but they won't last long in the apocalypse."

"It takes more than righteousness and conviction," Edna agreed. "It's about practicalities. And the right balance between ferocity and compassion."

I glanced at each of them and smiled. "I'm glad I'm in your bunker, ladies."

Keats gave a yip of agreement and we all laughed.

CHAPTER TWENTY

I was still hanging around with Wilma and Byron when Jilly came
to collect me from the barn later in the afternoon.

"I figured I'd find you here," she said. "You might as well bring a
sleeping bag down and spend the night."

"Good idea," I said. "It would save time going back and forth to
the house. Plus I get to avoid Mom."

"I heard that," she called from the doorway.

"I counted on it," I said.

"Please tell me you are not going to this event dressed like that,"
Mom said.

"I'm totally going to the event dressed like this," I said. "There
are things I dress up for, like dates and certain parties, and then
everything else. This is in the everything else category."

"Ivy Rose Galloway, I brought you up better."

"You brought me up differently," I said. "I'm quite sure you
didn't intend for me to become a farmer, but it all worked out."

"You have a skewed perspective on things. Honestly, Ivy. You
just got your stolen pig back."

"I know. Isn't it grand?" I turned to look into the pen where
Wilma was contentedly scouring her trough while Byron dozed in

the straw. He seemed exhausted from constant vigilance, whereas Wilma had come home revitalized. She had given Keats a merry chase when he brought her in, but all Byron had to do was give a rumble, and she did his bidding. "She is a new pig. A happy pig. She makes these little noises I've never heard before. Piping squeaks."

"Piping squeaks?" Mom said. "I'm going to sit in the truck and leave Ivy to you, Jilly. Your success rate at getting her to do anything is far higher than mine."

"I don't want to leave them," I said, after Mom stomped off. "What if something happens?"

"That's why Poppy offered to stay behind," Jilly said. "She's just getting her things together and she promised to text every half hour with photos of the happy twosome." When I still didn't move she added, "The mayor will expect to see you there, Ivy. And we want to stay on her good side, no?"

I sighed. "When exactly did I become such a yes-man?"

"The exact moment you went into business," she said. "Although I'd argue we've been yes-women since we started our careers. We're just yessing different things now."

"I'm not dressing up for these people. They don't deserve it."

She handed me a garment bag. "I chose this outfit with great care. It's just enough to look respectful to the mayor while still flipping the bird at the network executives."

"Really? We have outfits like that?"

"Of course. If you go looking like farmer Joe it will be cliché. If you dress up too much it'll say you're open to red carpets." She gave me a little shove. "Into the empty horse stall for a quick change."

I was laughing before I came out. Where Jilly had found a sweater with a big rubber duck on it was beyond me. It said everything and nothing, which is about what I wanted.

"I love it but I still don't want to go," I said.

"You don't want to miss this. The whole town will be on edge, torn between sucking up to the TV execs and insulting them. So often we have to hear about this kind of thing secondhand."

"I just don't want them to think I have any interest in what they're planning," I said.

"They're just doing a call for auditions today, from what Becky said on the phone. I cannot wait to see who raises their hand." She started herding me to the truck with Keats' help. "And Kellan will be there."

"There is that," I said. "Even if it's in his chiefly capacity."

"The execs can't bug you too much when he's attending in uniform," she said. "And there's the added bonus of making half the women jealous."

I grinned at her. "While you and Asher make the other half jealous."

"It's good to be us," she said, grinning back. "Most of the time."

When Poppy came down from the house, I put the truck in gear. "I'm worried about Poppy, Mom. Her spark is gone. How long since you heard her talk smack to you?"

"Too long," Mom said, with a sigh. "My heart aches for her, but if she'd just listened to me and started a healthy rotation, this wouldn't have happened. She pinned her hopes on Ray after mere days when she could have been wined and dined by several eligible men and never given him a second thought."

"She would still have felt betrayed that he used her to gain information," I said. "He basically pretended he didn't know her. It was cold."

"I know how hard that is better than anyone," Mom said, letting Keats climb through the seats and curl up in her lap. If she was willing to be seen by TV execs covered in dog hair, she must be sincere. "That's why I advise keeping many eggs in your basket unless you have a man of true character." She stared out into the evening gloom and absently stroked Keats' ears. "I used to think they didn't exist, but I raised one and you found another."

Jilly reached over and squeezed her shoulder. If I tried that move, Mom would have cringed or maybe even lashed out. But Jilly, her later life adopted daughter, and Keats, the grand-dog she didn't want, provided comfort I couldn't. On the other hand, I brought both into her life, so I still got some points.

We drove the rest of the way to Clover Grove Elementary School in silence. It was a strange place to hold a meeting like this, but probably the only space big enough on short notice.

Walking into the gymnasium brought an unexpected wave of nostalgia. I may never have been a schoolyard favorite but I had won nearly every academic award offered and that set the stage for who I became. Seeing Edna on the other side of the room, I thought about vaccination day and shivered. I could never have imagined then what we'd accomplish together. Both of us had certainly changed.

At the front of the room two men sat on a low wooden podium in front of the stage. They wore sports jackets over their open-neck shirts and jeans—a combo that said arty bigwig, I assumed. One of them wore a beret.

"Are you kidding me?" I said. "No one does berets in real life."

"Probably bald," Mom said, with a little smile. "He's keeping his head warm in a small-town winter." Jilly and I started to snicker and she shushed us. "Quiet, or I won't be funny. At least intentionally."

Edna migrated around the room to join us. "This is going to be such fun."

I thought about the old Edna pulling my brother out from under the stage by his feet and marveled at how she could be practically giggling. Granted, there was still a sadistic edge, but she truly was fun, now.

Asher didn't think so. Normally he was fighting a smile even in uniform but he stood as far away from the stage as he could and his expression was even more dour than Kellan's. I exchanged a quick smile with my boyfriend before his chiefly frown reappeared.

"Take a seat, everyone," the man with the beret called. "Let's get started."

We stayed at the back of the room, leaning against the wall while people rushed to get seats in the front rows. There was a lot of flapping and twisting as they tried to wedge themselves into the child-sized seats. Heddy Langman actually slid off and took the chair with her. Kaye helped her up and both women flushed.

"Oh, the poor darlings," Mom whispered. "I'll remind them of that the next time we try to pin a murder on them."

I covered my mouth. "Mom, stop it. You're going to get me in trouble in school."

"It wouldn't be the first time, darling. The principal called me in often to rebuke me for lax parenting."

Mr. Beret introduced himself as Stan Ellis and his bespectacled companion as Dex Bocker.

"Thanks for joining us today to salute Vivian Crane, who left us so tragically this week." He signaled Ray in the front row, who pressed a remote. A screen came down over the stage and Vivian's face appeared with dates underneath.

"Oh, please." Mom whispered. "She was born earlier than that. By a decade."

"Stop," I hissed. "Respect for the dead."

A greatest hits reel played soundlessly while Stan enumerated some of Vivian's credits, and then segued gently into talking about the show, Faraway Farm.

"As you know, the premiere had aired before Vivian passed," he said. "It was an immediate hit but we can't go on as we'd expected, obviously. Vivian *was* the show."

Sounds of relief and disappointment collided over the crowd and pretty much cancelled each other out.

Stan raised his hand for silence. "Fear not, the show *will* go on... just not as it was. We're going with an entirely new format that focuses more on humor than the quiet elegance Vivian was known for. Our producers are in discussions now, but the leading and supporting roles are currently up for grabs. We'll be in town for a couple of days holding auditions and I hope to see some of you come out."

Excited murmurs crashed into clucks of disgust, and Heddy Langman, still flushed, raised her hand. When Stan nodded, she called out, "The people of Clover Grove don't care to be the butt of your jokes, Mr. Ellis. Your crews have been intrusive already. We value our privacy here."

"Speak for yourself," said Dina Macintosh, the owner of the Hound and the Furry. "This production can bring business to all of us, including you, Heddy."

Teri Mason managed to get out of her kiddie chair despite being hamstrung by a flowered caftan. "I agree with Dina. I'm happy to host you at Hill Country Designs, although of course, we'll all want to sign waivers."

Mayor Martingale was standing near the front and she stepped forward. "You raise a good point, Teri. I think everyone's concerned about being portrayed as..."

"Country bumpkins," Edna called out. "Or yokels."

There was a gurgle of laughter, and Teri chimed in. "We're okay with people laughing *with* us, but not *at* us. There are lots of good people in this town trying to do the right thing."

"I hear your concern," Stan said. "But we also know what tests well with our audience. They want simple and heartwarming, which Clover Grove delivers by the truckload. But they also crave a little slapstick. These are difficult times across the country. You can be the thing people look forward to each week. The thing that is guaranteed to put a smile on everyone's face. Can you do that for the nation?"

This time more people murmured yes than no. He was making it a civic duty to become a laughingstock. And the mayor wasn't protesting for us.

I raised my hand. Someone had to speak.

Mom tried to pull down my hand and we had a little tussle.

On the stage, Stan and Dex both laughed. "Yes, that's perfect. Just what we're looking for! We can always count on you, Ivy Galloway." He signaled Ray again. "On that note, let's flip to a highlights reel that shows rather than tells you our vision."

Before I could say a word, the screen on the school stage filled with denim. Baggy denim overalls. A baggy denim butt, to be precise.

My baggy denim-clad butt. I would know that butt anywhere.

There was a joint gasp of horror from Mom and Jilly as they identified the butt as well. Edna was grinning, and Kellan, when I dared to look at him, had looked down at his boots. My brother, on the other hand, lit up the room with his smile.

After the close-up, they cut to a montage of my greatest pratfalls. It opened with me getting dragged backward by the donkey over the cobblestones in town square, then cut to me slipping on manure, falling over a fence, being mowed down by Drama Llama and finally, getting flattened by Wilma. That shot had been taken the day of Evie's visit to pitch her own show. It was a different angle, so I knew they'd been spying on me even then.

The highlights reel ended with a close-up of Wilma's wild-eyed face, clearly framing her as the villain of the piece.

Everyone turned in their child-sized seats. All I could see in that moment was mouths hanging open in laughter.

Jilly clutched my arm and whispered, "Eight count. Starting now."

I couldn't breathe at all. My head spun, my throat seized and my chest hurt.

"I'll get Kellan," Mom said. Her voice sounded far away.

"No." I got that word out and then another. "Keats."

Jilly bent over and the dog was in my arms with his muzzle pressed against my neck. He murmured one sympathetic sound and then followed it with a string of canine profanity that infused life back into me.

"Don't you cry, young lady," Mom said.

I shifted Keats to look at her. "Oh, I won't. I'm going to invite them for coffee."

CHAPTER TWENTY-ONE

S tan and Dex were sitting together on one side of the booth when I arrived at the Berry Good Café. They didn't know they were sullying "my table" with Kellan.

Or did they? Turned out they knew plenty more than I thought. I suppose Jasmine, the young blonde waitress wringing her hands behind the counter, had probably told them in exchange for a cameo.

"Hey, guys," I said, walking over and sliding onto the bench across from them. It was a tight squeeze in my bulky parka but I didn't plan to stay long.

Keats gave them a cool-eyed stare, sent all his alarm flags flying and then obeyed my request to move under the table. He leaned heavily against my shins. Maybe he was a third of Byron's size but his presence was massive.

"We're so pleased you asked to see us," Stan said. "We've been eager to talk but Meryl Martingale discouraged it."

It made me feel slightly better that the mayor had kept them at bay.

"Listen, I'll cut to the chase," I said. "I'm going to keep Byron. Do you remember his original name?"

"Byron?" Dex asked, peering at me over his glasses.

"The show's dog. The one that ran away. Or was stolen." His expression was still blank, so I continued. "Clearly you won't miss him if you don't remember him. But I found and rescued him today when I went looking for my pig. The murder weapon was there, too, in case you hadn't heard."

The men looked at each other quickly, and Stan adjusted his beret. "I don't think anything's been proven."

"Sure it has," I said. They thought I was a rube—a country butt-kin—but I knew a thing or two about bluffing. "It's only a matter of time before the press shares that Vivian Crane was killed by a network anxious to avoid a very expensive contract."

Hearing a man in a beret shriek was exactly what I needed to feel better after my public humiliation.

Before he could say anything, Keats gave a warning bark and I looked up to see Becky Bower walking into the café. She gestured for me to make room for her on the bench and I said, "Sorry, Becky. This is a private meeting."

"Private? Who are you to—?"

"Private," Stan echoed. His voice was far less strident now. "We'll speak later."

He flicked his fingers and her face furrowed like a raisin before she turned. Under the table, Keats panted a ha-ha-ha.

"What is that noise?" Dex asked.

"My dog. I mean, my other dog. Now I have two, thanks to you."

"Our production dog is pedigreed," Dex said. "If it's the one I'm thinking of. An Anatolian shepherd."

Jasmine finally came over and I ordered a coffee and refills for the men.

"Caucasian shepherd," I said. "It's a generous gift from you to Runaway Farm to make amends for the damage you've done. It might stop me from suing you."

Dex laughed. "For what?"

"For having cameramen trespassing on my property and airing private footage without my permission."

"You can't prove that," Stan said, relaxing now. He was getting his sea legs.

"I can, though. I have security cameras that will show Ray and Eric lurking in the bushes. I know exactly where they were to get that shot."

"Ray was invited onto your property," Stan said with a smug smile. "By your sister."

"Not that day. And not with cameras. It's our word against yours and with that murder problem, I think my word will win."

"That's utterly ridiculous," Stan said. Yelled, really. He hadn't noticed that the seats nearby were filling quickly as people spread the word we were here.

"Do you really want to raise your voice, Mr. Ellis? Because the town grapevine is incredibly fast and annoyingly inaccurate."

He leaned across the table and hit me square in the face with breath far worse than that of any rescue animal I'd met. Even Hollywood wasn't immune to halitosis.

"Young lady," he whispered. "I suggest you stop impugning our network. We will not hesitate to bring the full force of our legal team down on you. You have nothing."

"I do, though." I gave him my very best HR smile: no teeth, just lips pressed in the small arc of doom. The one I used when I fired someone for cause. "I have proof you wanted Vivian gone over your contract dispute."

"Contract disputes are all in a day's work in our business," Dex said.

"Plus there were complaints about her bullying and harassment," I said, taking a wild guess.

"Again, just typical business. Someone always hates someone else who makes more money."

"But you were at risk of losing good people over this."

Dex shrugged. "People come, people go. We're all replaceable."

"Is there a team for that?" I asked.

"For what?" Stan asked, finding his voice again.

"For making people go. Permanently."

"No," Dex said, "but there's a legal team that delights in addressing specious accusations."

"They used to call me the grim reaper of HR," I said. "Maybe you've got one for real."

"Keep that up and you will lose your farm," Stan said. "You can't leave our butts hanging out to dry."

"Why not?" I said. "You just left my butt hanging."

"You're really willing to lose your pig and your cows and whatever else you've got in that menagerie?" He leaned even closer and I had to hold my breath to stand his. "We will take your dog. The one chewing my jeans under the table. You will always wonder what happened to him."

"Can you say that again?" I lifted my phone from the seat beside me. "I'm not sure I caught it."

He swept off his beret and flung it across the café.

"Stan, chill," Dex said. "We'll just give Ivy what she wants and this will all go away. Like it always does."

Stan sat back and crossed his arms.

"Thanks, Dex," I said. "You seem like a reasonable man and I'm not an unreasonable woman. My list is quite short, really. I want Byron. He makes my pig very happy."

"Done," he said.

"I want you to leave me alone. No cameras, no phone calls, no offers. Nothing. Stay away from my family, and friends—furry and otherwise."

"Done," he repeated.

"Then we're good," I said, slapping some money on the table to cover my coffee. "I just want to go back to leading the quiet life. Do I have your word?"

He held out his hand and I dropped the phone in my pocket before I shook it.

Stan crossed his arms and looked away.

"Don't be like that, Stan," I said. "Your show will go on without me."

"It most certainly will," he said. "You can count on it. And you haven't heard the last of us."

"No threats, Mr. Ellis. The chief of police hates that."

"I wouldn't count on him covering your butt," Stan said, with a nasty laugh. "It's a liability to him."

I shrugged. "Maybe. He seems to like it though. Gotta run. I really appreciate your time."

Stan dropped a few bombs under his breath as I slid out of the booth and snapped my fingers for Keats.

I was halfway out the door before I realized Keats was carrying something in his mouth. The remains of a beret.

Grabbing a few mints from the bowl, I went back to the table and set the beret in front of Stan.

"Sorry, Mr. Ellis. I'll replace that for you." I rained the candy down in front of him. "In the meantime, have some mints."

Keats panted a ha-ha-ha as we left. I smiled and then sighed.

"That was just one battle, my friend. We still need to win the war."

CHAPTER TWENTY-TWO

I stalled twice on my drive through town the next morning. My bravado had disappeared overnight and now I was more than a little unnerved by the network executives' threats. Who was I—farmer Ivy—to take on the big guys? I didn't have evidence that they'd done anything to Vivian. It was just the drunk ramblings of bitter cameramen.

However... however...

Ray had been right about Vivian being in a dispute with the production. They had wanted her gone. Were they willing to take extreme measures to do it? People got fired and replaced in Hollywood all the time. It was just a matter of money.

Or did the execs convince the crew to do the deed for them? I had seen so many bullied employees snap over the years, including a fatal episode at my own farm. If they were worn down enough, the execs could have shoved any of them over the edge.

Another possibility was that Vivian had something on them that they didn't want revealed. Only Becky would know that, I figured, and that's what I wanted to find out today.

Keats mumbled some encouragement as I started the truck again in front of Miniature Mutts. A few people gathered and waved. The pratfall highlights reel was dancing in their eyes. We'd all be seeing that for a long time. It would go viral online, if it hadn't already.

There was another mumble from Keats to confirm it had. No doubt Mom and Jilly had closed ranks to keep me from knowing for as long as possible.

"Never mind that," I said. "We're going to focus on Becky right now. She'll have her guard up, to say the least. It will take all our wiles to get her to talk." I glanced at him doubtfully. "I don't think my wiles go that far."

He panted some encouragement, but I could see the doubt in his blue eye, too. I had no more tricks up my sleeve and Becky was smart enough to know it.

"Let's just see how it all plays out," I said. "Strange things happen sometimes. You know that."

He pounded his white paws on the dashboard in a blatant "bring it on."

That lifted my spirits enough that I didn't stall again until I pulled into the parking lot at the Faraway Farm set.

"What the...?"

I was more puzzled about what I didn't see than what I did. Specifically, there were no vehicles at all.

"Have they left? Oh please, tell me they've left town for good."

Keats didn't look convinced. In fact, his ears were back and his ruff up. He didn't like the atmosphere here one bit. No surprise in that when the Swenson farm had been steeped in crime and abuse for generations. I didn't believe in ghosts and evil spirits, but if such things *did* exist, they'd find plenty to feed on here.

"On the off chance they've pulled up stakes and gone, I'd better check on the livestock," I said. "Sadly, I wouldn't put it past them to leave them behind. Poor white critters."

Keats was subdued as we walked up the driveway and around the house. I felt the weight of the stories here and maybe he did, too. At least it was broad daylight. At least we were together.

The cute little red barn looked as bright and perfect in the weak morning sunshine as it had the first day I saw it. It was like a dollhouse for animals. I wanted one to play with. Keats gave me a look and I shrugged.

"I'm too practical to get one, but I'm still a girl, Keats. I like cute things."

He grumbled something like "let's get this over with" and I didn't argue. If there was any trouble with the livestock, I'd call in Dr. Roxton immediately and stay till he arrived.

By the time I reached the barn, my worries had eased. The horse was standing at the doorway, chewing a mouthful of hay. Healthy and happy.

"Hey girl," I said. "Where are your buddies?"

There was a movement behind her and Chess, the farmhand, came out. He tipped back the brim of his Stetson and smiled. "Well, good morning. If you came to see the crew, they've shipped out."

"Shipped out? As in left? For good?"

"Don't sound so happy." His smile turned to a grin. "Because they're just having an offsite meeting in the city. One of the head honchos flew in and the police chief let them go."

"Darn. You got my hopes up."

"You may get your wish," he said. "I never count on anything in this business. It's like a traveling carnival. You arrive, try to get settled but not too settled. Then you wait and see if the show wins or loses." He shrugged. "This one may lose but the game ain't over yet."

"Well, I'm glad you're here, anyway, because I wanted to talk to you."

He beckoned me to follow him into the barn. "Can't take my eyes off that goat for one second or she's eating something she shouldn't. Yesterday she managed to climb right up on top of the barn. Threw my back out getting her down." He looked around and shook his head. "It's designed for looks, not practicality."

"I thought the same thing when I was admiring it earlier."

Peering around him I saw the white goat gnawing on a broom handle in the corner. "Oh no! That splintered wood can't be good."

I started over but he stopped me. "My bad, I got it." He walked over and gently pried the little goat's mouth open and took the broom away. "She's a handful."

"What you're kindly not saying is that I've taken her babysitter away."

His eyes crinkled. "You didn't take Byron away. He got away from the crew. Then you found him and took him to a good home. I'm not complaining about that. Just about the mischievous goat. He kept that girl in check. Felt sorry for him sometimes, though."

"He's got another challenging girl now. My pig is a trickster. One minute she's wallowing, the next she's running like the wind."

"Glad you got her back. How far did she get?"

"Miles from here, which is even further from my place. I couldn't believe it when I saw them together. They were perfectly happy. Didn't want to come home."

He looked a little sad and for a second, I wondered if I'd made the right move. "Is he settling in okay?"

"Beautifully. He's a wonderful dog and I'll have plenty of work for him, besides Wilma. I bet you love him, too."

"He's a real good dog. But like I said, you try not to get too attached in this business. Places, people and animals come and go."

"I promise I'll look after him well. Would you like to come and see him?"

He shook his head. "Don't want to disrupt him again. We weren't together long, anyway."

"I understand. Is there anything I can do to help?"

"Yeah," he said, smiling again. "Take the goat."

I'D HAD some quirky passengers in the back seat of my truck but the small white goat was the most trouble. She was small, agile and very determined to drive. Keats was equally determined to keep her from taking the wheel. She tried every trick in the book to get over, under and around him and he fielded every assault, even if it meant going after her from my lap. Eventually he nipped and she bleated. Even then she persisted. She simply would not take a telling and Keats wasn't used to that. Never was I so happy to drive under the familiar arch to the farm. Amazingly, I hadn't stalled once or hit the ditch. I was that focused on getting home.

I backed the truck right into the open area of the barn to make sure the goat didn't make a run for it when I unloaded. After Wilma, I was being extra cautious.

As I set her hooves on the ground, she collapsed, attacked my boots and then slithered away from me. My hands caught thin air but for once I got lucky. She did the exact opposite of what I expected and jumped right into a pen. Specifically, Wilma's indoor pen, where the pig herself was lounging with her new boyfriend.

I worried Wilma would take offense but she didn't even bother to lift her head. Byron got to his feet, sniffed the bouncy, frenzied little creature, and then crashed in the straw again. The goat climbed on top of him and went to sleep instantly. It was like the dog had hit her "off" switch.

"Nicely done, Byron," I said, trying to tie the remains of the bootlace the goat had just torn off. "You're hired. Again."

"Did I just see you driving with a goat in your lap?" Kellan was behind me, and he didn't sound amused.

I froze, hands still on my boot. "No. She was never in my lap."

"Well, she was everywhere else and Keats was fighting her off from your lap. She was a wildcat."

"She's young and exuberant," I said, pulling out the whole bootlace. "It wasn't that bad."

"I followed you for a mile, trying to decide whether to pull you over. It seemed like it might do more harm than good."

"I appreciate that," I said. "Because I'm sure someone would have caught it on video and that would have gone viral, too."

I was still bent over showing him exactly what he'd seen on the big screen at school yesterday, but I didn't particularly want to face him, either.

"Ivy. Can you leave this boot crisis for a minute and talk to me?"

"She ate my lace. I'm trying to fix it."

He came over and knelt in front of me. "I'll do it. You're worn out from being trapped in a moving vehicle with a feral goat."

"Thank you. I am." Straightening, I left the reins in his capable hands. "Keats was fed up. Look at him."

The dog who never napped had climbed onto a hay bale and collapsed. It was probably the first time he hadn't greeted Kellan with audacity.

"Maybe it's better not to take your baby goats for a drive," he said, threading the remains of my lace through the eyelets. "Some animals make better travel companions than others."

That made me laugh. "I won't do that again," I said. "But Chess Cochrane unexpectedly asked me to take her for a week."

"Chess?"

"The livestock wrangler at Faraway Farm. I went over to apologize for keeping Byron. He was fond of the dog."

Kellan glanced up at me skeptically. "You went over there just to talk to him about the dog?"

"No one else was there. I heard you let them leave town."

"Did you also hear Asher went with them? No one's going anywhere unsupervised until this case is solved."

"Fine. I went over there to see if I could wrangle some information out of Becky."

"As if she'll open her heart after you threw her out of the café yesterday."

"Oh, you heard about that?"

"Calm cool Ivy lost her temper, or so I'm told. Jasmine doesn't hold back anymore."

"I lose my temper plenty when there's an animal involved. No one cared the dog went missing. They didn't know his breed or his real name."

He pulled the lace out and started over. "That doesn't make them murderers, Ivy. There's no evidence to suggest any of them are implicated. Trust me, I've looked. They were at loggerheads with Vivian, but lawyers would have sorted that through eventually."

"Maybe not fast enough. Especially if they could get me for cheap." After a pause, I said, "Well, who do *you* think it is, then?"

"I'm working through my process, like always. It may not be fast enough to please the mayor, but it does get me where I need to go."

"She's given me a bit of grief too," I said. "Wanted Keats and me to do some digging."

Kellan sighed, fiddling with the laces. "I figured, although she denied roping you in. I hope she realizes she's putting you in a precarious situation."

"She does. At the risk of sounding cynical, that's what politicians do, under the guise of serving the public first. I worried her support for the inn would dry up if I didn't try to help."

"You'd do it anyway," he said.

"Probably, since my animals are at risk. But I don't like to be told what to do anymore."

"Tell me about it." Finally, he laughed a little. "I guess those network execs know that now, too."

I got mad all over again. "They're slimy and despicable, and they don't deserve a dog like Byron."

"Do you really need a second dog when the first one is perfect?" he asked, sounding relieved to change the subject.

"Byron is specialized. He's a pig whisperer and I'm sure he's going to settle those thugs down, too. He's got magic calming powers."

"How does Keats feel about that?"

"Ambivalent. He may be glad to offload some grunt work if Byron doesn't try to muscle in on the fun stuff. My guess is they're so different they're compatible."

"So you brought home two new animals in less than a day?"

"The goat's temporary and I won't even name her."

"You could try convincing the network execs to let you keep her by accusing them of murder again. That's a good strategy to get their goat."

"Funny. But I needed that dog for Wilma, and it was a fair exchange for humiliating me in front of the entire town."

"It wasn't that bad," he said. "And it was only half the town."

"The camera crew skulked in my shrubbery and spied on me. Plus they made Wilma look like a crazy wild boar."

He sighed as he deftly wove my bootlace. "She is crazy sometimes. And there have been worse videos online."

I stared down at his hair, which was unruly from his hat but still somehow perfect. My fingers ached to touch it but I didn't. "I hoped you didn't see them."

"They're hard to miss, sweetie. And I'm only human. I need a laugh, too."

Embarrassment surged from my boots to the crown of my head. The endearment barely took the edge off.

"I'm sorry," I said. "I know you must get teased about them. About me."

His hands stopped moving and he looked up. "Ivy, no one would dare tease me about you. Do I seem in any way teasable to my staff or the citizens of Clover Grove?"

"I guess not. But they would if they could."

He laughed. "How about we not worry about woulds and coulds? There are so many legit things to worry about." His fingers started lacing again, making sure it was perfectly even. "As if I would care what anyone said anyway. You should know that."

"Let's drop the shoulds, too."

"That's pushing it. There are some important shoulds on the table. And should nots. Like you should not drive with a goat in your truck. That's a good one. And it's the law."

"There's no law saying you can't drive with a goat in your truck. I'm sure I'd have heard about that."

"Maybe you could spend less time turning manure and more reviewing the laws of our highways."

"That's a could and a should all wrapped into one," I said. "When driving without goats is just common sense."

"There you go," he said, smiling up at me again. "You're good to go down here, too."

Somehow he'd managed to tie my boot good and tight on two-thirds of a lace. I stared down at him and said, "This might just be the most romantic moment of my life."

His smile was warm enough to melt the snow off the barn roof. "I can do better. It's almost Valentine's Day."

As he braced himself to get up, a ball of orange fluff plummeted from a stall and landed between his shoulder blades. Percy was gone as fast as he came and Keats took his place, having recovered from exertion with his usual speed. He stood on Kellan's back like king of the castle.

"Off, special constable Keats," Kellan said, straightening slowly so the dog could drop to the floor. "Those two are the exception to my rule. They dare to tease me, when they could and they should find someone else to torment."

I took his hand and walked him out to the police SUV. "You deserve better."

"Than them? Maybe. Than you? Never." Turning me to face him, he ran his hand over my goat-ravaged hair and plucked out some straw. "Could you and would you try to be a little more careful, please? This will be my first Valentine's Day that actually means something… providing you last that long."

I stood on the tips of my laced boots and kissed him. "No more driving with goats. I promise. Surviving to Valentine's Day is a very worthy goal."

CHAPTER TWENTY-THREE

I had screamed before—probably more than many in their entire lifetimes—but never had a screech ripped out with such intensity that it practically took my tonsils along for the ride. There was a moment where I knew what it was like to fly, because I actually did soar through the air. Then it all ended with a hard thump as my helmet knocked against a tree stump.

"That shriek ended your singing career," someone said. The voice sounded far away because of the helmet. "Good thing you've got a donkey to cover for you."

"Edna, shut it." That voice belonged to Jilly and it was a lot closer. I opened my eyes to find her bent over me. Only her green eyes were visible through the visor of her own helmet. "Are you okay, Ivy? Is your head okay?"

Another face loomed over me and a wet nose touched my visor. Keats whined and stared at me with his brown eye. The canine energy transfusion got me on my feet in short order.

"I'm fine," I said. "Did you really need to drive that fast, Gertie?"

"No," she said. "I just *like* to drive that fast. Don't you?"

"Ivy's a plodder," Edna said, from the seat of the blue snowmobile—the one that had belonged to Gertie's husband. "That's why we're driving, Gertie."

Jilly helped me back into place behind Gertie. "Are you sure you're able to go on?"

"Absolutely. I just lost my grip when Gertie hit that last bump. Also, I keep getting whacked in the face with her braid. It's like a serpent."

Keats panted anxiously at my side and I gave him a pat with a heavy waterproof mitten to prove I was ready for action.

Putting her hands on the hips of her bulky snowmobile suit, Jilly glared at Gertie. "Ivy is still recovering from a head injury, in case you weren't aware. Getting conked again could be catastrophic. Maybe we should switch drivers. I'm fully capable of piloting this machine."

Gertie laughed. "You'll toss her again in three minutes. Do you want that on your conscience?"

"Jilly, I'm good," I said. "Gertie knows the terrain better than anyone. All she needs to do is slow down."

"That's no fun," Gertie said. "Life is short, ladies, you've got to enjoy the ride."

"I couldn't agree more," Edna said. "I learned that too late but I'm making up for lost time now."

"Just get us there in one piece," I said. "I made a promise to Kellan to live till Valentine's Day. This probably wasn't what he had in mind when he asked me to be more careful."

Edna lifted her visor and grinned at me. "If he wanted a woman who wrapped herself up in an afghan to cross-stitch, he'd have picked a different sister. There are other Galloway options."

"Stop that," Jilly said, swatting Edna as she climbed back on board. "It's a sensible request from a sensible man."

"He does seem well aware of Ivy's demons," Gertie said.

"Demons?" I propped my feet on the running board. The

hardest part was maneuvering bulky gear on a streamlined scream machine. "What demons are those?"

"The ones that drive you headfirst into danger with your eyes wide open," Gertie said. "Don't get me wrong. I consider that a personal strength. Not everyone does."

"It puts you first on the list for my bunker," Edna said. "Just what you need in an apocalypse. I'll be sure to stock plenty of helmets for you."

"I can't zap zombies wearing a helmet," I said. "They'd get me from the back or the side. Plus I'd never hear them coming."

Jilly tossed me a grin before lowering her visor. "Keats and I will warn you. Zombies are not subtle."

"Deal," I said, dropping my own visor. "Hit it, Gertie."

The next leg of our journey was staid in comparison to the heady first run. I missed the speed. Riding so fast and so low to the ground was exhilarating. Keats enjoyed racing alongside, too. I realized that busy as he was, he rarely got to run full out and he was still a young dog. Maybe I should get us a snowmobile.

"There," Gertie said, when we reached our destination. "Safe, sound and bored."

I pulled off my helmet and set it on the seat. "Can I drive on the way back?"

"No!" The word came from three women and one dog.

"Oh, come on. I'm a good driver without a stick shift. In most conditions."

"Which do not include a blizzard coming in," Jilly said, pulling off her helmet. She held out her arm to show the snow accumulating on her black sleeve. "Let's do this and get back to that hot cocoa Gertie promised."

Gertie and Edna lifted their visors, leaving their helmets on. The warriors remained ready for immediate deployment. In fact, Gertie bent to release Minnie, her rifle, from its compartment on the side of the snowmobile. "If Finch and Starling show up, I'm serving roast bird for dinner."

"Ugh, don't even," Jilly said. "This is a peaceful mission."

"Until it isn't," Edna said.

Our brigade of five headed for the old barn where Wilma and Byron had been contained. The fences were gone after the police investigation and the footprints of the team had been covered in a fresh coat of snow. The barn itself looked sad and even more derelict without the animals, and the door that hung askew looked like a gaping mouth.

"You really think the police missed something, Ivy?" Jilly asked.

"I promised Percy I'd check. It's a shame we couldn't bring him, but it wasn't safe. At least Keats could take care of himself."

The dog panted a yes-yes-yes. He was actually giddy with excitement over the run.

We were nearly inside before that changed. His lashing tail did a stop and drop. His ears flattened. And everything that could puff, did puff.

"Uh-oh," Gertie said, raising her rifle. "I'd better stay back and guard the perimeter. I can't get a good shot inside with a rifle."

"I'm kicking myself for not bringing my pistol," Edna said. "All I have is pepper spray. I'll need a trailer for the skidoo to carry my kit."

"I'm sure it's fine," I said. "Keats didn't like the vibe here before and it was empty. We'll just take a quick look around and go."

"Make sure it's not booby-trapped," Gertie said. "By the Pefferlaw boobies." After a moment she called, "Are boobies birds of prey?"

"Seabirds," I called back, pulling off my big mitten and groping in a zipped pocket for my phone.

Jilly got hers out, too, and we walked into the barn in twin beams of light while Edna cocked her canister of pepper spray. The energy was all wrong here and I understood why Keats was on red alert. But our army of five was strong and steady.

"So where was Percy when you left?" Jilly asked.

"In the rafters. Right about... here." I stood in the corner and pointed. "Boost me?"

"Are you kidding?" Jilly said. "I can barely move in this suit. We'd both come crashing down."

"How else can I take a look? It felt like I could fly earlier but I'm just a projectile."

"I'll bend over and you can stand on my back," Edna said.

"Edna! Your discs could collapse and I'd be down one general," I said. "Jilly can lift me on her shoulders. She's done it before."

Jilly glared at me. "Uh, no. I'd remember that."

"Must have been a dream," I said, grinning. "But you're always the wind beneath my wings."

"Okay, I'll try it once," Jilly said. "If we fall, I'm out."

"We won't. As soon as you're upright, I can grab the rafters and pull up. It'll only take a second to look around."

Jilly bent over and I locked my bulky snowsuit-clad legs around her shoulders. It would likely have been a failure to launch had Edna not been there to help Jilly straighten and balance. She even pushed my butt up from behind to take part of the load. Eventually I was aloft like an unlikely blimp.

Keats whined from what seemed like far below and I called down, "It's okay, buddy. I'm good."

"I'm not," Jilly grunted. "Less talk more search."

I shook off my other mitten so I could grip the top of the wall with my left hand while aiming the phone into the small space between the wall and the sloping roof. My heart sank as I saw there was nothing.

"Nothing?" Jilly echoed, as if I'd said it aloud.

"Nothing. Except a wee bit of straw. Cops must have cleaned the whole place out."

I plucked at the straw and stuck it in my pocket. It wasn't good for anything but I felt like I needed to come down with something after Jilly had risked her neck for me. Literally.

She lowered me on my signal and her flushed face looked elated rather than annoyed. My city girl twin had also come a long way in the adventure department.

"Bupkis," Edna said as we left the barn. "Don't you love that word?"

"It's good one," Gertie said. "But we're not leaving empty-handed, if that's what you mean."

"Why? What did you find?" I asked.

She pointed at prints. They were reasonably fresh, based on the amount of snow we'd had, and one just under the eaves was pretty clear. It was large. Very large actually, and it obviously belonged to a man.

"What's that?" I asked, pointing to a neat little circle beside it. "There's another one here. And here."

Edna looked at Gertie and shook her head. "Oh, to be so young again."

"I don't get it," I said, gesturing for Keats to take a good sniff. There would be little he could pick up with the snow falling, unfortunately.

Gertie tipped her rifle butt up and pressed the business end into the snow. Then she pretended to lean on it. "Get it now?"

"A cane! Someone was here using a cane."

"Or just a regular walking stick," Edna said. "Either way, it probably wasn't Finch Pefferlaw. He looked like he could take down a bear."

"Maybe someone came armed with a stick to fend off a bearlike dog and a pig," I said. "And discovered they'd been claimed."

"Well, we won't get answers standing around," Gertie said, revving the machine and starting to move forward. "Save the chitchat and let's roll on these tracks. They're filling in fast."

It was a shame visors didn't come with wipers because the

driving snow pretty much blinded me as Gertie followed the tracks as best she could. She couldn't see well either, but fortunately our canine soldier had the advantage. He wove in and out of tight spots we couldn't reach and waited as we caught up. I was sorry we couldn't give full-out pursuit yet relieved I wouldn't go flying again. Better to live to fight another day.

Gertie slowed and I lifted my visor. "Fresher," she said. "He's not far ahead of us, and slower."

Edna gave a whoop that would have fogged her visor. "Get that man and I'll trounce him with his own cane."

So close. We were so close. And Keats showed every sign that this was a key person of interest. A dangerous person.

And, unfortunately, a smart one.

Just a few yards later, the prints ended abruptly at the fastest running creek in the area.

"Dagnabit," Edna called, swerving this way and that. "No telling which way he went. Could have doubled back for all we know."

"Divide and conquer?" Gertie asked.

"No," I said, and Jilly echoed the word from behind her visor. "No dividing the brigade."

"It's our big chance," Edna said. "No guts, no glory."

"If there's one thing I've learned, it's that trouble circles around to find me," I said. "We'll get another chance."

The older women shook their heads at each other in disappointment.

"They're not making girls like they used to," Gertie said.

"We'll leave them in the bunker to ripen," Edna said. "Soldiers get better with age."

I couldn't help but smile. That was something I never believed in my old life, where the corporation ruthlessly targeted midlife staff for redundancy. Out here in farm country, the wisdom and experience that came with age were prized.

"Hit it, Gertie," I said. "This young old lady wants to sit by the fire with her cocoa."

CHAPTER TWENTY-FOUR

I took my time closing up shop that night. Egg collecting in the morning and bedtime barn rituals framed my day in a predictable and soothing way. If those went well, it mattered less what happened in between. Seeing Keats' plumy tail bobbing ahead of me down to the barn early and back up late bookended a good day —even if it wasn't a perfect day. No day on the farm went according to plan. There were too many moving parts. That was one thing I loved about it. In my old life, I was an expert in making things go to plan and my motto had been "No surprises." Here, I could barely make it through an hour without a surprise great or small. But morning and evening tended to be bombshell free.

Tonight my biggest worry was whether or not to give in to Wilma's insistent pleas to spend the night in her outdoor pen. After two days inside, she was getting bored with the cushy life. A dog's love, it turned out, was not enough to make up for fresh air. I had to move the goat in with the sheep in case Wilma took out her frustrations on the innocent.

"I don't know, girl," I said. "I worry about you being outside."

She offered an unusual series of chirps, snuffles and squeals. A sow soliloquy.

"You're making a good case," I said, "and I know your boyfriend has regular predators covered. It's the human pignapper we need to think about. I'm not sure Byron could scare him off."

Byron moved over beside me and stared into my face. His normally placid dark eyes were intense. I couldn't read him properly yet, but the message he vocalized in a deep rumble was loud and clear: "Outside."

The two animals stood side by side watching me. Never in my memory had Wilma deliberately tried to meet my eyes. She really wanted this, and I had promised to listen and try to make her happy. I couldn't go back on my word.

"Okay, here's the deal. You guys can spend a few hours outside and I'll bed down here in the horse stall with Keats and Percy. If anything goes wrong, we'll know about it instantly."

The two animals let out overlapping cross-species approval. It was interesting to hear their mingled dialects. Normally they were quiet together, so I assumed the babble was for my benefit.

Keats added his voice to the conversation, only he wasn't happy.

"I thought you'd like to camp out here," I said. "You spend the night at the window anyway. Now you can be on site, with all the comforts my sleeping bag can provide. I'll wear the snowmobile suit."

He continued to complain all the way up to the house and all the way back. The return was slower as the puffy suit was meant for getting tossed in a snowbank rather than strolling with an armload of supplies.

"This is a bad idea," Poppy yelled after me from the porch. "Jilly wouldn't like it."

"She deserves the night off from supervising me, Pops," I called back. "Don't you dare rat me out while she's enjoying her date."

"Then let me stay out there instead. I'll call you if anything happens."

I stopped and made a slow turn, like a grounded blimp. It wasn't like my sister to make an offer like that. "That's really sweet of you, but making my pig happy isn't your job."

"Maybe I'd rather be down there with fifty animals than up here alone. Mom and Jilly won't be home from their dates for hours."

"Just lock the door and keep your phone handy. You'll be the first person I call if there's trouble."

"After Kellan, you mean."

"And Edna. But you're first after them."

She laughed. "Fine. Stay warm."

I turned the blimp around and started moving again. "This suit is overkill. I'm about to explode."

"Sounds messy," she said, still laughing as I went into the barn.

After dumping my things in the vacant horse stall, I unlocked the outdoor pen, did the same with the indoor pen and told Keats to move Wilma and Byron. It was his first time herding the huge dog and I worried they'd clash, but Byron either respected their different livestock roles or didn't care. I had to trust that he'd live up to his breeding in case of real threat. He seemed more like a living teddy bear than a natural killer.

"Satisfied?" I asked, locking the gate behind them. Wilma raced around the outdoor pen squealing with what certainly sounded like joy. Now she was truly home. I assumed they would ultimately bed down in the insulated shelter I'd filled with plenty of fresh straw. Their body heat would keep it toasty.

Walking back inside, I said, "Maybe I should get her a coat. Do they make pig jackets?"

Keats offered a withering comment that was more about his own coat, that he now had to wear all night. These cold days, he was often only free of it at bedtime.

I debated about locking the three barn doors—front, back and side. It would keep trouble out but would slow me down if something went wrong. Ultimately I compromised and locked the back but kept the side door to the pig pen open. Then I lumbered to the main door at the driveway and was surprised to see lights coming down the lane.

"Someone's home early," I said. "Mom's date must have gone bust."

But the sedan that pulled up was familiar and when the window rolled down, I saw the blonde, highlighted hair of Mayor Martingale.

"Sorry to come so late, Ivy, but my days are full lately."

"Plus you don't want to be seen," I said, smiling.

"That, too." She returned the smile. "Is that thing comfortable?"

"Nope, but I'm winter camping. Wilma and her new boyfriend wanted some fresh air."

Her brow furrowed. "Is that wise when neither you nor your boyfriend have located Vivian Crane's killer?"

"I've done all I can," I said. "I'm quite sure the network hired someone to rid themselves of an expensive contract negotiation. Stan and Dex admitted they were locked in a dispute with Vivian."

"That doesn't mean they'd kill her. They have more money than they know what to do with, so they'd have settled eventually."

"Eventually doesn't work for men like them. They had a good thing going over at Faraway Farm and wanted to make the shift to someone new as soon and as seamlessly as possible."

"Sounds like speculation," she said. "Do you have any proof?"

"Just the camera team's account of rising tension. She'd been called on the carpet many times and there was yelling. Any of the crew could have done it of their own volition or as network puppets."

"Not buying it," the mayor said. "Is that snowsuit making you lazy, Ivy?"

"Maybe. Or maybe I promised my boyfriend to let him do the heavy lifting on the detective front. He's a longtime graduate of Ordeal School, whereas I'm still a novice."

She blinked at me a few times as if evaluating my sanity. Making people wonder was one of my key strategies.

"Ivy, far be it from me to understand why the network wants you starring in their show after you accused Stan and Dex of murder in public, but I'm here to tell you that it's still the case."

I closed my eyes. "That's impossible."

"In their own words, they're like the Terminator. They just keep getting right back up. And for some reason they want you on board. Maybe it's because you're resilient like that, too."

I laughed despite my incredulity. "Well, I guess they just want to keep close tabs on me. It's sweet of them, but no."

"Not even for the good of Clover Grove?"

"Declining this show *is* for the good of Clover Grove. You must have seen that in the school auditorium. We were just starting to pull the town together with our Culture Revival Project and now the show is tearing us apart with secrets, games and manipulations. I want this town to thrive but it won't through that particular show."

"You could negotiate with them to shift the focus to something more unifying."

"Negotiating got Vivian killed, it seems. The only thing that unified people about this show was seeing me take pratfalls. Flattering as my popularity is, I'll stick to rescuing animals and building goodwill one book or knitting club at a time. I hope you'll still support Runaway Inn, but if you can't I'll find my own way."

"Of course I'll support you," she said. "You're a good person, even if we don't see eye to eye on what's right for this town." She put the car in reverse and started coasting. "Besides, my niece would have my butt in a sling if I said one harsh word about you."

"Wait," I said. "I'll let you gain some points with her."

"Always welcome," she said, hitting the brakes.

Kneeling beside Keats, I smiled. "Take my photo in this suit. She'll love it. And believe it or not, I trust her not to put it online."

"You can trust me, too," the mayor said, pulling out her phone. "But be careful, okay?"

"We always try." I raised a bulky sleeve as she drove off, then looked down at Keats and sighed. "Usually we fail but it's the effort that counts, right?"

He offered a grumble that sounded more worried than sulky as I started pulling the double doors closed.

"What's wrong? Should we check on Wilma and Byron?"

Passing back and forth in front of me, he mumbled more that I couldn't pick up. "Slow down, buddy. My brain is overheating in this thing and might blow a circuit."

I was pulling the door closed when I saw light in the lane again. A truck this time. It was probably Asher's pickup and I was a bit relieved they'd decided to come home early. Having my brother on site was almost as good as Keats.

The dog offered an indignant yip.

"Almost," I said, out loud. "If you're going to eavesdrop on my thoughts, listen closely."

The truck that came into view was unfamiliar and had a trailer in tow. Turning smoothly, the driver backed the trailer right up to the barn.

When the door opened, I was surprised to see Chess Cochrane, the livestock manager from the Faraway Farm production.

"Hey, Chess," I called. "Did you come for your goat? Because you're welcome to her. I've never seen a more hyperactive animal."

"Giving her caffeine was a mistake," he said, laughing. "But she's your problem now. Better be more careful with your offers, Ivy, because you just won the horse lottery, too."

"Seriously? That's amazing!" It wasn't amazing that I was getting a second horse—third if you counted little Clippers. But if he was dispersing his livestock it could only mean the production was folding, despite the mayor's plea.

"One horse, one sheep, coming right up," he said, looking around. "You're going to need a bigger ark, Ivy."

I laughed, as if it were the first time I'd heard it. "I need a bigger budget. I have the land to expand but can't build for awhile." I raised one hand. "And no, I don't need to hear that doing the show would have financed that."

"No reproaches from me," he said. "I'm good with moving on, like the old carnie I am. This show felt cursed." Blowing out a sigh, he added, "Not that I believe in things like that."

"Me either," I said, smiling. "But the old Swenson place had a toxic history dating back a century. Generations of animal neglect and abuse. I'm sure a handler like you could feel that in your bones."

He rubbed his back. "I sure feel something in my bones. Climbing after that silly goat tore a muscle or two. I'm not as young as I used to be."

"It's a shame you're not staying in Clover Grove longer," I said. "People get better with age here."

"Tempting," he said, turning to open the trailer. "But not tempting enough. I want to put all this behind me."

"Wait," I said. "Before we offload the new kids, let's go out and see Byron. He'll be excited to see you."

"Byron doesn't do excited," Chess said. "He's the calmest dog I've ever known, and I've wrangled a lot of them."

He followed me through the barn, definitely moving more slowly today. Either his back really was bad or the show had sapped his life force. Or both.

My phone rang and I groped around till I remembered which of the many zippered pockets held it. Seeing Kellan's name, I raised a hand to Chess and said, "Have a word with your pesky goat while I take this, Chess. She's in with the sheep because she revs up the other goats."

He walked over to the sheep pen and leaned in. The movement must have hurt because he braced himself on the gate.

"Hey there," I said, into the phone.

"Ivy, if you're in the barn you need to go up to the house now. Lock the doors."

"Oh?" I slipped into my neutral HR tone on a dime. Mentally, I pulled a lever and several images popped up at the same time. Three lemons all lined up in a row. I was a winner, but the prize wouldn't taste like lemonade. One casual glance around confirmed it. Chess had picked up one of the three pig pokers, with its long wooden handle and the iron hook on the end. He was leaning on it, like a man who'd taken a long walk through the snow and a creek... with a cane. My fingers twitched instinctively for the piece of stiff straw I'd found in the old barn's rafters that morning. Now I realized it came from the broom used to sweep away tracks after Vivian died. Kellan had likely come to the same conclusion when the police found it, which is why he was calling now. And last, I remembered seeing something odd in the bushes when the mayor showed me the video the crew had taken of me walking into the pond. It was a Stetson, low to the ground, perhaps bent over a dog.

My eyes shifted to Keats, who was standing just outside the pool of light in the doorway between us and the pig pen. And if ever his posture had sounded the ding-ding-ding of a slot machine, it did now. "Well, I'm sorry to hear you can't come over," I told Kellan with the poise of long practice, "because I wanted you to meet my new horse. Chess Cochrane just stopped by with the rest of the livestock from the show. They're folding up their tents and rolling on."

"Chess is there right now?" His voice had a note of alarm. "Do you know that—"

"Yep, Keats is in a state about it. He doesn't like surprises but he'll keep things calm as we get the new additions settled."

"I'm coming," he said.

"I can't wait for Edna and Poppy to see this horse. She's a beauty."

"Texting them now," he said.

"Great. See you tomorrow."

I slipped the phone in my pocket without hanging up.

"Sorry about that, Chess. The news went over like a lead balloon, I'm afraid. My boyfriend thinks I need a bigger ark, too." I gave him a carefully modulated HR smile. *Never let them know you know* was another one of my old mottos. "He'll come around like he always does. The more the merrier. Now let's go see Byron."

Chess stumped after me, leaning heavily on the pole. I wanted to be outside, even though there were animals to worry about on either side.

"Hey, boy," Chess said, walking up to the fence. And then, "Wow."

Inside, the huge dog had puffed to resemble a bear and his fangs were showing.

"How strange," I said, unlocking the gate quickly. "Something must have spooked him. I'd better check things out."

Keats took my cue and scooted inside ahead of me, and I closed the gate.

I always wondered why Charlie had put a lock on the inside, too, but I was glad of it now.

"I wouldn't shut yourself in there if I were you," Chess said.

"Why not?" I asked, smile still holding.

He smiled, too, and it had a look I'd come to know well. Feral.

"Because it leaves me out here with the rest of your animals." He glanced toward the inn. "Plus the lady stepping out of the house."

I unlocked the gate and opened it. "Come right in, then."

CHAPTER TWENTY-FIVE

The invitation left Chess in a bit of a quandary. Did he want to come inside with a guardian dog that apparently considered one of us a threat? Or did he want to stay outside where he had leverage? He didn't hear the motor in the distance, but I did. More importantly, Keats did, and he went through the gate, circled Chess and made the decision for him. The old man gave a screech and jumped forward, with a sheepdog hanging from his backside. Once the man was inside the pen, Keats backed out and shoved the gate closed.

I was on my own now, with an aggressive dog, an erratic pig and a man with a very good weapon.

"So, what did you want to talk about?" I asked, slowly maneuvering until I was between him and Wilma and Byron. "You came over for a reason."

"I came over to give you the animals, that's all. You turned it into something else."

"All I did was put the right pieces together at the wrong time," I said. "I really wish I figured out you'd killed Vivian *before* you got here. Or after. It would have been more convenient."

"You're telling me. I could be on the road to Wyoming right now instead of stuck in a pig pen with a problem."

"You could still get on the road. Drop the hitch to the trailer and get a head start."

He looked like he was thinking about it. "The police are coming?"

I shook my head. "Missed my chance. So you take yours and run. But before you go, can you please just tell me why?"

"The bigger question is why *wouldn't* someone kill Vivian Crane?" he said. "She was a disrespectful bully who treated people below her like dirt."

"Above her, too," I offered. "She would have been fired eventually if you'd let things run their course."

"Couldn't take that chance. After the premiere, I knew the show had legs. And that meant fighting Vivian night and day for months or even years to defend these animals. This is the fourth dog she hired and fired. The third goat. The second horse. The only original standing is the sheep. And each time the animal was dumped on whoever would take them. Like they didn't matter at all. It was abuse, and it didn't stop there. 'Spare the broom, spoil the mutt,' is what she said. When she whacked Byron for being 'a dullard who sheds,' something snapped in me. Too many productions have treated too many animals like dirt." He paced back and forth, twirling the pig poker like a baton. "They brought in a Caucasian shepherd and Vivian punished him for having fur. It was only a matter of time before she broke this calm dog and he turned on others. I couldn't protect him."

"She was even worse than I realized," I said. "Sounds like putting her down was the right thing to do. But why then?"

"I was out searching for your pig and ran into her jabbing Wilma with a stick. Trying to herd her, she said. As the head poop-scooper, I had a shovel and a broom with me, like always. So I used the first and then the second. I hid in the bush with the pig. She came willingly because I'd dropped food for her the day before."

"You released her?" I asked.

He shook his head. "That was Eric. Becky sent him during the launch party. To throw you off your game." He shook his head. "Pig could have died or harmed others, so I tried to help."

"Thank you," I said. "It's too bad things spiraled out of control."

"To the point where I was stuck in the bushes feeding crumbs to a pig while you're in a pond. Then you found the glove and I had a bigger problem. When Becky dropped Byron's leash, he came to me and we skedaddled. The old barn was a lucky find."

"It was perfect," I said. "Wilma was happy there."

"I'd have gotten them into good homes before long, but you had to go poking around."

"It's a weakness," I said. "Everyone says so."

"Now, here we are."

"Here we *were*," I said. "Because you'd better skedaddle."

"Knowing what you know, I can't just leave now."

"Chess, you've got to leave now. Otherwise you're forcing the dog you wanted to save to defend me against you. He doesn't want to do that. Both animals like you. Don't make them choose."

"They won't choose you. I saved them."

"They will." The confidence in my voice came from a deep knowing. "We're already a team. A family. Listen to me, Chess. Hear me."

He didn't listen. Instead, he swung the pig poker. Luckily I had experience with that particular weapon. I dropped to my knees and it zoomed right over my head, throwing him off balance.

Wilma did the rest. She ran hard into his shins and he crumbled like old timber. I heard a terrible crunch—a broken bone, perhaps—and she came around for a second charge.

"Wilma, no! Keats!"

I remembered he was outside the pen. And yet, there he was circling around me to have what appeared to be a meeting of minds with Byron.

The dogs split off. Keats cut in front of Wilma and herded her into the corner. Byron stood over Chess, fluffy paws on the man's chest. His fangs showed in a terrible snarl, but at the same time, he whined.

"Look what you've done," I said. "You've broken this dog's heart."

"Well, your pig's broken my leg, so it's even."

"It's not even. But it is over."

"Not yet," he said, groaning as he reached into his coat and pulled out a pistol. "But soon."

The roar of the ATV cut out as Edna pulled up close to the fence and then jumped inside. She let out a war cry that got his attention and raised her crossbow. "Let me do the honors."

"Or me," Poppy called from the open gate, where she stood with the ax from the woodpile. "Time to cut down a bad guy."

"He's not a bad guy," I said. "He just wants to kill me."

There was no need to fight over the opportunity anymore, because Chess' gun dropped from his hand as he passed out.

I wasn't far behind but Byron left the unconscious man and offered me his broad back as support. Keats still had his paws full with Wilma, who seemed determined to finish Chess off. Mercy was a foreign concept to this pig.

"Breathe," Poppy said. "In for six, out for six. Just like Jilly says."

"Get her out of here," Edna said. "I'm going to cuff this guy."

The sirens were close now. Edna dropped her crossbow, flipped the unconscious man and snapped cuffs onto his wrists.

"Byron, go deal with Wilma," I said, and snapped my fingers for Keats. The bigger dog did exactly that, swiftly backing Wilma into her shelter and blocking the doorway. He could move plenty fast when necessary.

Kellan paused in the doorway of the barn, took everything in, and let his men surge around us. I walked out and into his arms while Asher—in his civvies and obviously fresh off his date—pulled Edna out of the pen.

"Don't make me carry you again, Miss Evans," he said. "Because I will do it. And my fellow officers will film it and post it online."

"Viral sensation," one of the other cops called. I had no doubt he was a survivor of Edna's vaccination program, too.

Edna dropped her resistance and followed Asher into the barn.

"Is that a crossbow?" Kellan asked as she passed. "An illegal weapon we agreed I'd never see?"

She dropped it into the empty pig stall and offered empty hands. "How is that any worse than Poppy wielding an ax?"

"It's worse," Kellan said. "I'll count the ways for you later."

"You do that, Chief," she said. "And all the while I'll picture the stoic little boy I—"

"Edna," I said. "Cease and desist. You could be using that energy to help me open the scotch bottle."

"Well. Since you put it that way." She followed me away and Poppy pulled up the rear as we headed for the house.

"I could use a drink," Poppy said. "Deciding whether or not to let Keats back in nearly killed me. If he'd been hurt..."

"He wasn't. You made the right call, Pops." I smiled at my sister and forgave her for what happened with Ray.

Edna winced over the sisterly emotion and changed the station. "I bought a snowmobile," she said. "I like the sleek lower profile."

"Why am I not surprised?" I said, turning to call Keats.

The dog paused in the barn doorway with pleading eyes, both blue and brown.

"Okay," I said. "Stay and help Kellan. But don't be too long, okay? I need you."

He mumbled something sweet back and Edna shook her head. "You two are sickening."

"Can I drive your snowmobile?" I asked.

"Maybe," she said. "How good is the scotch?"

CHAPTER TWENTY-SIX

Jilly made whiskey sours. She said she needed to do something constructive with her hands, and when I told her about my mental image of a slot machine lining up clues like lemons, it gave her the idea to start squeezing.

I unzipped the snowsuit, rolled it down to my waist and sat at the kitchen table. All the juice had drained out of me, but it would come back. It was a constantly renewable resource, like manure.

"It's always been your favorite cocktail," Jilly said. "So we need to rescue it from the memory of that dinner party with the camera crew and make positive associations."

Poppy had been pacing over the kitchen tiles, but now she dropped into a chair next to me. "Pearl onions," she said. "How are you going to salvage those?"

"How about a blind date?" Jilly asked. "We've got a few connections, now."

"You're in luck, Poppy," Mom said, from the doorway. "I've just set up a date for you."

She'd gotten back from her date a few minutes after the police took Chess away, which meant we were spared additional theatrics.

"No," Poppy said. "I can live without pearl onions."

"Pearls are a girl's best friend," Mom said. "So I've set up half a dozen dates for you. It's critical to have at least six good men in a rotation to avoid overinvesting in any of them. And because math was never your forte, I'll add that it takes about three or four times that many dates to get six solid matches. It's truly a numbers game, Poppy."

"Mom, she wouldn't have energy for my farm work if she went on that many dates," I said. "It sounds exhausting."

"Do I look exhausted?" She swept a hand from her red lips to her red suede boots. "I had two dates back to back because I'm down to five in my regular stable. The key is that they must all be equally amazing. Then if one fizzles, you just fill up the calendar again. It's hard work at first but you train for it. It's so fun getting to know new people."

Poppy and I both laughed. Mom had never been a worker bee but in midlife had found the twin passions that motivated her— dating and barbering. Now she set a great example for those that came after, even if it bypassed our generation.

"I need to take a little 'me time' and recover first," Poppy said. "Maybe spend some time on Ivy's manure pile."

"Absolutely, darling," Mom said. "Take all day tomorrow. Your first date isn't till the evening. We're meeting one of my favorite gentlemen and his son at The Tipsy Grape. If all goes well, you could have something lined up for Valentine's Day."

Poppy looked at Edna. "Is your crossbow still in the pig pen?"

"Don't be silly," Edna said. "I went down and collected it while Kellan was busy with the perp. He confiscated my last one and they are not cheap."

"Do you mind if I target practice on Mom?" Poppy asked.

Edna studied my Mom, who studied her back. "Nah. Dahlia has her challenges, but she produced good candidates for my army. After the uprising."

Mom crossed her arms. "I'll be in that army, Edna Evans."

"Not if your only talent is running in heels," Edna said. "There are no heels in a bunker."

"I'm very good with a straight edge," Mom said. "Very good indeed. How many others can say that?"

"Few," Edna admitted. "All right, your space is secure, Dahlia."

Mom looked inordinately pleased, and I realized that like me, she was probably chosen last for every team. Her small size meant she'd be more of a liability than an asset. But on Edna's team she'd be prized.

Jilly and I looked at each other and shook our heads. Sometimes it was hard to know whether to laugh or cry in this kitchen, on this farm. She brought over a highball glass clinking with ice and raised hers in a salute to me.

"Ah..." I said, smacking my lips. "Lemons for the win."

"Congratulations, darling," Mom said. "For taking down another dirtbag."

My mother had never used that term to my knowledge and I peered at her over my glass. "You know, Mom, it's complicated. I wish all criminals were completely despicable but there's a lot of nuance. I try to understand them, even if their actions were wrong."

"That's where our HR and recruitment training comes in so handy," Jilly said. "We see the nuance."

"And that's where an apocalypse comes in so handy," Edna said. "Things go back to good versus evil. No energy wasted trying to see both sides."

"A zombie is a zombie is a zombie," I said. "Refreshingly simple."

Edna sat down and raised her drink to mine. "You'll need to learn to shoot while riding a snowmobile and ATV."

"What about skydiving?" Poppy said. "I've done that a few times. And cliff jumping. Ziplining. Kiteboarding. For starters."

Edna glanced at her quickly and with new respect. "Poppy, I

thought you were the least ambitious Galloway Girl, but I couldn't have been more wrong."

Mom's hands went to her hips. "Poppy Galloway, are you crazy? You could have been killed."

"Any number of times," Poppy said. "Which is why I never mentioned tombstoning, which is what we called it in my adventure club. Now I see my experience could be an asset in some situations."

"Someone else in the family inherited the daredevil gene," I said, smiling. "It surfaces late for some of us."

"The environment in Clover Grove is just right for it," Edna said. "There's something in the water."

Mom joined us at the table and we all clinked highball glasses again.

Percy selected Mom's lap because the fabric of her red dress was lovely and soft. And when Keats came in with Asher, I scooped the dog up onto mine.

He mumbled an excited version of events down at the barn, and after Asher stooped to kiss Jilly's cheek, he said, "The dog's not wrong. It was lively. That Stan guy with the beret? Screaming so loud you could hear him clear across the country."

"Tell me it's over," I said. "That the network is truly closing down Faraway Farm."

"Done. Gone. All you got is the livestock," he said. "I unloaded the horse and the sheep for you, by the way."

"Wilma and Byron?" I asked.

"Sound asleep in their cabin." He held out his phone so that I could inspect the photos.

I waved it away. "I need to go down to the barn anyway. Bad memories stain more if you don't rinse them out immediately."

"I'll join you," Jilly said, dropping Asher's hand and getting up.

"Thank you, my friend," I said, squirming into the snowsuit again.

"Can I come?" Asher said.

We shook our heads in unison.

"Girls' night," Jilly said. "Pops, pour the man a drink. We'll be back soon."

"Officer Galloway," Edna said, as we went out the back door. "What skills do *you* bring to a zombie apocalypse?"

CHAPTER TWENTY-SEVEN

"I'm shocked you'd let me bring you here," Kellan said, pulling me closer. "You're not the girl I thought you were, Ivy Galloway."

"That's just it," I said. "It's Valentine's Day, so I turned into a real girl for one night."

"You most certainly did."

There was no mistaking the admiration in his voice and while the color rose from my rather low neckline to my face, I held my ground and smiled up at him.

Directly behind his head was a mirror ball and the flashing facets made it somewhat dizzying. For a second I thought they might trigger one of my migraines, but Kellan spun me around just in time. He threatened to dip me and I squealed a protest. It brought back visions of my mom in her ballroom dance craze.

That's exactly why we were here at the Palais Royale, however. Jilly's notion of cleansing bad memories and attaching new associations was a good one—and necessary at the rate we were going. Clover Grove wasn't that big a town and we needed to get out sometimes without being reminded of past traumas.

Jilly certainly didn't look traumatized as she whirled around and around the dance floor with my brother. He was a surprisingly good dancer for a former football star, but Kellan was even better. I wanted to ask where he'd learned the steps but zipped my lips. Some things were better left as a mystery.

"Half the town is here," I said. "From teenagers to long-married couples." Edna, Hazel Bingham and Martha Kinkaid sat on the side-lines, taking a turn on the floor when someone asked, and plenty did. "I love the community spirit. This is what we need more of, not TV shows."

"You're preaching to the choir," he said. "That production brought nothing but trouble and I couldn't be happier we've lost the spotlight."

"And yet my highlights reel lives on forever," I said. "It's nice that it starts and stops with a close-up of my butt."

"This dress is far more flattering. I don't want to share it, though, so please don't bend over. If you drop your handkerchief, I'll pick it up."

"Deal. I wore it for you and you get to call the shots."

He laughed. "Perfect. Then how about I take Hazel and Martha out for another spin and we call it a night?"

"What about Edna?"

"Ivy, I can't," he said. "Ask me anything except that. Cleansing those childhood memories is going to take more than a waltz under a mirror ball."

"Understood. I'll go say goodbye to the others and get our coats."

While Kellan danced with Martha, I wove through the crowd, enjoying the laughter and music.

Suddenly I hit a pocket of what felt like frosty air. Keats wasn't here to confirm my intuition but I knew instinctively that someone was up to no good. Looking around, I saw Beverly Roxton sitting with the Langman sisters.

"Good evening, ladies," I said, stopping at their table. "Enjoying the dance?"

"Not particularly," Heddy said. "Your mom has commandeered all the men, which leaves some of us idle."

I gave them an innocent smile. "Would you like me to ask Kellan or Asher to do the honors?"

"No thank you," Heddy and Kaye said together.

Kellan and Asher might be the most handsome men in the room but they were also too close to the law for the Langmans' comfort.

"Well, goodnight then," I said, heading on my way. I stopped to chat to half a dozen others who were far more receptive to my overtures. One by one, I'd rehabilitate this town, till we were functioning like a well-managed rescue farm. All it took was listening—and truly hearing—what people had to say.

Well, that wasn't all, but it was a good place to start. If it worked on Wilma it would work on most critters.

A middle-aged man in a nice suit stepped out from behind a pillar and grabbed my elbow. "We need to talk," he said.

"Do I know you?"

"Not yet, but you will," he said. "You need to help me so that I can help you."

"Oh?" His nails were digging into my bare flesh and I wished my sheepdog were here to back the man off. "Perhaps a Valentine's gala isn't the time for business."

"It's always time for *this* business," he said.

"I'm just on my way out, I'm sorry."

My philosophy about listening and hearing didn't extend to strange men grabbing my arm. It was time to drop my metaphorical handkerchief.

Kellan was on the dance floor with Martha, but when he saw my look he passed her to my brother and joined me quickly.

By that time, the man was already gone. Kellan's reputation clearly preceded him.

"What was that about?" he asked.

"I'm not sure. But I have the feeling I'm going to find out."

"Do you want me to follow him?" Kellan asked.

I shook my head and smiled. "No way am I letting this dress go to waste. Let's take it home and have another dance there. I enjoyed the evening but I'd like to be alone with my Valentine. Or at least as alone as we can ever be at the farm."

"We'll never lack for company," he said, collecting our coats. "But your mom will dance till the very last song."

The door closed behind us, shutting off the music and chatter and even a new mystery. I looped my arm through his and we walked down the stairs into the breath-snatching cold. Now the night was truly ours.

Do you want to try my other mystery series? The SECRET series that's hidden in plain sight?

Sign up for my newsletter at **ellenriggs.com/opt-in** to find out how you can read the first in the 11-book series for free. There's a little more romance, a lot less murder and plenty of heartwarming humor.... plus a large cast of mischievous mutts. My newsletter is full of funny stories and photos of my adorable dogs. Don't forget you'll also receive the free Bought-the-Farm prequel, *A Dog with Two Tails*.

RUNAWAY FARM & INN RECIPES

Jilly's Classic Beef Stew

- 2 lbs stewing beef
- 2 tsp flour
- ½ tbsp of salt
- 1 tsp black pepper
- 1 ½ tbsp coconut oil (or other cooking fat)
- 1 large onion, finely diced
- 1 large carrot, minced
- 1 celery stock, minced
- 4 cloves garlic, minced
- 6 tbsp tomato paste
- 2 bay leaves
- 1 tsp dried thyme
- 1 cup red wine (or 2 tbsp balsamic vinegar)
- 2 cups chicken broth
- 1 lb mini potatoes (or 4 large potatoes cut in 2-inch chunks)
- 1 lb peeled pearl onions (optional)

Pat beef dry with paper towels. In a large bowl, mix flour, salt and black pepper. Add beef and toss till coated.

Heat a Dutch oven or large, oven safe pot over medium-high heat. Add the oil and then the beef, allowing it to brown on all sides. As it browns, move the meat to bowl. (Don't crowd the beef!)

When all the meat is browned and removed, add minced onion, carrot, celery and garlic tot the pot and cook till golden, about 10 minutes. Add the tomato paste, bay leaves and thyme. Cook, stirring often, about 2 minutes. Pour in the wine (or vinegar) and the broth and mix well. Then add back the beef and juices. Cover and simmer for an hour on the stovetop or put it into the oven at 375 degrees for an hour.

Add the potatoes and pearl onions, if using. Continue to cook for another hour or so, until the meat, potatoes and pearl onions are tender.

Remove lid and simmer on stove uncovered for about 10 minutes to thicken the gravy. Season with more salt and pepper to taste. Garnish with parsley if desired.

(Chef's note: Need a man to confess... or profess his love? This lip-loosening meal will increase your odds. It tastes even better and is equally powerful the second day.)

More Books by Ellen Riggs

Bought-the-Farm *Cozy Mystery Series*

- A Dog with Two Tales (*prequel*)
- Dogcatcher in the Rye
- Dark Side of the Moo
- A Streak of Bad Cluck
- Till the Cat Lady Sings
- Alpaca Lies
- Twas the Bite Before Christmas
- Swine and Punishment
- The Cat and the Riddle
- Don't Rock the Goat
- Swan with the Wind

- How to Get a Neigh with Murder
- Tweet Revenge
- For Love Or Bunny
- Between a Squawk and a Hard Place
- Double Dog Dare
- Deerly Departed
- Think Outside the FoxMouse of Ill Repute
- Bee All and End All
- Sheep with One Eye Open
- Roo the Day
- Till Death Zoo Us Part

Bought-the-Farm Mysteries - *Boxed Sets*

- Bought the Farm Mysteries - Books 1-3
- Bought the Farm Mysteries - Books 4-6
- Bought the Farm Mysteries - Books 7-9
- Bought the Farm Mysteries - Books 1-10

Mystic Mutt Mysteries *Paranormal Cozy*

- I Want You to Haunt Me
- You Can't Always Get What You Haunt
- Any Way You Haunt It
- I Only Haunt to be with You
- All I Haunt Is You (Novella)
- Do You Haunt to Know a Secret?
- All I Haunt for Christmas

Books by Ellen Riggs and Sandy Rideout

Dog Town *Series*

- Ready or Not in Dog Town (The Beginning)
- Bitter and Sweet in Dog Town (Labor Day)
- A Match Made in Dog Town (Thanksgiving)
- Lost and Found in Dog Town (Christmas)
- Calm and Bright in Dog Town (Christmas)
- Tried and True in Dog Town (New Year's)
- Yours and Mine in Dog Town (Valentine's Day)
- Nine Lives in Dog Town (Easter)
- Great and Small in Dog Town (Memorial Day)
- Bold and Blue in Dog Town (Independence Day)
- Better or Worse in Dog Town (Labor Day)

Dog Town *Boxed Sets*

- Mischief in Dog Town - Books 1-3
- Mischief in Dog Town - Books 4-7
- Mischief in Dog Town - Books 8-10
- Mischief in Dog Town - The Complete Series